haunted hearts

A SMALL TOWN ENEMIES TO LOVERS ROMANCE WITH A GHOSTLY TWIST

HAWTHORNE BAY
BOOK 1

LUCY VALE

*To every 90's girl who watched Casper and absolutely melted
when Devon Sawa whispered,
"...can I keep you?"*

This one's for you.

"I've spent so long in the darkness, I'd almost forgotten how beautiful the moonlight is."

EMILY, *THE CORPSE BRIDE*

one

WILL

There's beer soaking into the carpet when I walk into the living room, freshly showered but trying to get my tired, non-caffeinated ass out the door. On the couch is my brother, Zeke, empty beer cans strewn around him and a string of spit hanging out his mouth. He's passed the hell out.

"Seriously, man?" I say, not even caring if I wake him up.

Actually, on second thought, he *better* wake up. It's the third time in two weeks he's come home wasted and slept 'til noon, and even though I love the fuck out of him, I'm not running a daycare here.

"Mm," Zeke groans. He rolls over onto his back and slings a long, tanned arm across his face. "Turn the light off, Will. My head hurts."

I snort. "The only light that's on is the sun, you dumb fuck. Come on—time to get up. You're not going to lay around again all day."

"Man, you suck," Zeke says. But he pushes himself up to

a seated position anyway, then sits there blinking at me, a lopsided smirk on his face. "You should just admit you're jealous, and maybe I'll take you along next time."

I snort, kicking a beer can out of my way as I move toward the front door. "Oh, yeah? What am I jealous of exactly—getting kicked out of your apartment? Your headache?"

Zeke rests the back of his head against the couch and puts his feet up on the coffee table. This time, he grins for real. "Ha. A headache's a small price to pay for amazing head—"

He's cut off when I chuck an empty can at him, and it hits him square in the face. He bursts out laughing. "I don't want to hear about your exploits. I want you to get a fucking job."

"A *fucking* job? Like, where I get paid to—" This time he catches the can I've chucked at him, the flimsy aluminum cracking between his hands as he grins. "—fuck?"

"I don't care what you do," I bite out, dodging the can as he pelts it back at me. "Just get your shit together, alright? I've got your back, but you need to start pulling your own weight, dude. You don't see Benji and Phoebe showing up here, asking for handouts."

Zeke makes a face and falls back against the couch cushions, annoyed at the sudden mention of our other siblings and his shortcomings. He hates being reminded that I'm covering his student loan payments. "Yeah, yeah. I will. But really, this chick from last night? She's got an older sister—fine as *hell*—and I bet she'd be down for a piece of Will Holloway sometime. You're brooding as fuck. Women eat that shit up."

"I can get my own dates, thanks," I say. And it's true—I've never had any problems in that department. It'd be hard to miss the looks I get from women, even if it's been a while since I did anything about it.

Zeke gets up from the couch and makes his way to the kitchen, stretching his sinewy arms above his head. He switches on the coffee maker. "I'm just saying, Will. You might be a little less uptight if you let someone suck your dick once in a while."

He's not wrong, but I'm not about to tell him that. I'm a one track mind kind of guy, and right now, that one track has nothing to do with women or fucking and everything to do with the meeting I'm about to be late for.

Besides, even if I *wanted* something, relationships don't work for the men in my family. I learned that when my dickwad dad walked out on us twenty-two years ago, and the way Zeke's going, it looks like the apple doesn't fall far from the tree.

"There's a hot ghost that hangs out at the harbor," Zeke offers, and my head snaps around to glare at him. Zeke's grin is absolutely wicked. "If you *really* want no strings attached, I mean. Granted, it's been a minute since I—"

I scoff. "You know I don't fuck with that. That's all you, man."

"Oh, yeah." Zeke waves a hand. "You've got that wall thing going on."

"Yep. Thank Christ I do."

"You know, I still don't get how that works," Zeke drawls. He looks up at me, quirking an eyebrow as he chews a nail. "Like, I see these fuckers *everywhere*—and if I don't see them,

I hear them. They're always whispering and shit, like freaking snakes in my ear. Can't ever tell what they're saying, but I'm pretty sure half the time they just wanna know if their heels look good, or if I can tell their still-breathing ex to go fu—"

"I don't have time for this," I say, stalking once again to the front door as Zeke grins.

Zeke knows good and well that I worked hard to shut down the ghost-seeing part of myself years ago. He knows I know exactly what he's talking about too—all those creepy whispers and jump scares and asking favors—and that I decided I couldn't fucking take it anymore, that I didn't want anything to do with Dad and these weird-ass sixth sense abilities we so unfortunately inherited from him.

Not only that, but I've explained to Zeke several times how, after I made that decision, I spent *months* building up the mental strength to create an energetic wall around my mind that keeps me from having *anything* to do with ghosts. I told him about the hours I spent staring at my bedroom ceiling, gathering up all the little energetic wisps of myself and focusing them into a single laser beam of concentration. And when I got to the part about using that supercharged concentration to erect a shield—or a wall, as I usually call it —to finally free myself from the Holloway curse, this kid sat there and laughed at the word "erect".

So, yeah. No. I'm not about to rehash my wall with him.

"Anyway," I say, clearing my throat. I open the front door and glance back at Zeke, who's lounging against the couch cushions again. "In actual important news, I finally got approval on the basic plan for the library renovation—which means I've got to start in on design and won't be around to babysit. But Ethan Wilde's on the board, and if I can manage to impress him with this, there's a pretty good chance he'll ask me to design that development project he's been sitting on."

"Dunno who that is—but I hope you get it, bro."

Zeke flashes me a genuine smile, and for a minute, I can see the little kid I used to carry around on my back, galloping at full speed while he kicked me in the ribs. Zeke was just a baby when our dad peaced out, so the only father figure he's ever really known is... me.

Well, fuck.

As I hop in my truck and head off toward the center of town, I heave a sigh. I love my brother, but having Zeke here with me in Hawthorne Bay is... rough. Here I am, forgoing the new laptop I actually need so I can scrape enough together for those student loans, and he's passed out on my couch. Let's just say I'm starting to understand why his roommates back in Boston pulled the plug on him.

But honestly? Financial reasons aside, Zeke's behavior is just another reason to keep on pushing myself. Keep myself in line. It's been six years since Mom died. My brothers—and my sister—need *some* kind of responsible adult in their lives. God knows it's the least I can do, given it's my fault things ended up the way they did.

I may be one closed-off motherfucker, but at least I've got my shit together. And I need to keep it that way—for them.

But no pressure, Will. None whatsoever.

two

LYDIA

I've been waiting *months* for this meeting. With only 4,000 people in Hawthorne Bay, you wouldn't think it'd be so hard to snag some time with the director of the town's Historical Society. But here we finally are—and this woman, Eliza Corey, is staring at me across the town hall conference table with something that looks a little like pity.

"So there you have it," I say, putting on a cheerful smile despite the look on her face. I slide the binder I've prepared across the table. "I think it's really a no-brainer that the library is the perfect candidate for historical landmark status. Not only would it be a huge honor to the town—formally recognizing a building that holds so much history—but, with the right positioning, it'd also be a tourist draw for Hawthorne Bay. You know, a slice of New England lore and all that."

Mrs. Corey leafs through the pages in the binder, her pale pink nails gleaming in the overhead lights. I shift in my seat, waiting for her to say something. Throughout my pitch, she smiled and nodded politely, but I'd be lying if I didn't admit I was expecting more enthusiasm. As the assistant librarian, I'm probably biased, but the Hawthorne Bay library is one of the oldest buildings in town, and it's *beautiful*.

"Ms. Chandler," Mrs. Corey begins. Her fingers play with the edges of the binder. "I'll preface this by saying you make a compelling case. And the materials you've put together—the research you've done—is extremely thorough."

My heart sinks. She's saying all the right things, but there's something in her voice that tells me I'm not going to like what she says next. Mrs. Corey clears her throat and continues.

"That being said, I'm sure you're as aware as anyone of the renovation project that'll be kicking off in just a couple of months."

"Of course," I say, trying not to show the irritation that creeps in every time I think about that damn renovation project. I know I should be happy about it—renovating the library and all—but it means we'll have to close temporarily, moving operations to a trailer that Nancy, my boss, is calling The Bookmobile. Oh, well. It'll be worth the hassle in the end, having a nicer facility for the community. "Actually, I'm headed to the stakeholder meeting after this. I thought I could share with them the research I've put together, let them know the Historical Society's on board."

"Hmm..." Mrs. Corey rises from her chair. "I appreciate your enthusiasm, but my concern is that some of the plans for the renovation won't be compatible with the criteria for historical landmarks."

I stare at her, confused. "Won't be compatible? The

project may slow things down, but the library will be in *better* shape once everything's done. Besides, my understanding is that the plans are still being drawn up. There's still time to make sure everything's aligned—hence the stakeholder meeting today."

Mrs. Corey cocks her head at me. The pitying expression is back. "Ms. Chandler—Lydia—has anyone on the board... talked with you?"

"Talked with me?"

"Yes," she says. "I'm not sure it's my place to say anything, but I think there may have been some... wires crossed. Nancy Cohen is your boss, right? I'd suggest taking this up with her."

Mrs. Corey gestures to the door, and I follow her numbly out to the hallway. She hands me back the binder I put together, full of newspaper clippings, historical references, and photographs from throughout the years. As I take it from her, she pats my hand.

"I can tell how much the library means to you, Lydia," she says. "And if it were up to me, we'd preserve every facet. It's a beautiful piece of history."

The silent *but* hangs between us.

Mrs. Corey's face is kind as she holds the front door open for me. She tells me to take care, and I must say it back to her, but I don't remember because all I can think about is getting out of that building.

I stop on the corner, gulping in lungfuls of crisp, autumn air. Above me, the maple trees have begun to change color, their fiery leaves a burst of orange and red against the clear blue sky. For a moment, I close my eyes, willing myself to focus on the scent of salt drifting inland from the sea. I remind myself I've got this, that the world isn't ending.

Because honestly, even though it sounds dramatic, learning that something's going on with the Hawthorne Bay library—something I haven't been told about even though I *work* there—feels kind of like the world is ending. Or at least, like *my* world is ending. I feel like I've just been told my childhood home is being bulldozed.

Mrs. Corey said she could tell how much the library meant to me. And she's right—it does mean a lot. But she doesn't know the *half* of it.

She doesn't know it's the last place I spent a morning with my mom before we found out she was dying. I was ten that summer, and Mom—the head librarian back then—took me along with her to work that day. I sat cross-legged on the floor beneath the circulation desk, a pile of *American Girl* books next to me, and read while Mom worked. The library was pretty busy that morning, so we didn't talk much, but every once in a while I'd tap Mom's leg and she'd duck down to help me pronounce a word I didn't know. After lunch, I went along to the doctor with her, and when she came back out into the waiting room, her face was weirdly drawn. I don't think they knew for sure then that she was dying—she had to go back in for more scans, which is when everything turned into a blur—but I do know Mom didn't let go of my hand the whole drive home.

I remember thinking we never should've left the library. We should've stayed there, planted right at the circulation desk, for the rest of time. In the library, surrounded by the smell of books and the rustle of pages, life couldn't touch us.

I think about it every time I sit at the desk now, scanning books and looking up titles for kids like I once was.

Mrs. Corey also doesn't know how little Lydia Chandler, still trying to forget what it felt like when her dead mom's hand turned cold in hers, used to take down all the *Nancy Drew* books the library owned and curl up in the corner, reading them one by one. Her mom always loved *Nancy Drew*. Does she know how that same little girl would slide down the great wooden banister when the librarian who was no longer her mom wasn't looking, pretending she was a princess in a castle—whose father would be home that night, instead of at the bar? Does she know about the naps in the enclave? The hiding spots in the basement? No?

Then with all due respect, Mrs. Corey doesn't know *shit*.

Slinging my purse strap over my shoulder, I stride off down the sidewalk. Aside from the crunch of leaves beneath my heels, there's only the faint twittering of birds and the occasional rev of an engine. I pray I won't run into anyone I know because I'm going to need a few more minutes—and a giant ass cup of coffee—before I can get a handle on myself.

My sole coffee shop in Hawthorne Bay, Brewed Awakening, is buzzing when I get there. It's nine a.m., and half the town must have come for their morning cup of Joe because almost every single table is taken. I order my latte and go to stand at the far side of the counter, hoping the line won't take as long to get through as I fear. The stakeholder meeting starts in, like, five minutes, and I'll need to show up on time if I want to make a good impression.

My brain is a mess of racing thoughts, and the chipper conversations from the people around me aren't helping to calm me down. I'm not sure caffeine is going to help much either, but at least the act of sipping a warm, silky latte will be of comfort.

A buzz comes from my purse. Digging through it to find my phone, I check the screen and my heart sinks. There's still an unread text from Dylan—one I've been trying to ignore—but the incoming call that's flashing on my screen is *not* what I need this morning.

A quick scan behind the counter tells me the barista's not done with my latte yet, so I move away from the counter and answer my call. This had better be quick.

"Hey, Dad."

"Hey, hon. Just wanted to check in. How's it going?"

There's the faint blare of a TV in the background, and the clatter of glasses. I hope to god he's not at a bar this early in the morning.

"Oh, you know..." I pinch the bridge of my nose. Do I really want to go there with him this early in the day? Ah, what the hell. "It's not great, actually."

"That's good, that's good. Listen, I wanted to tell you... I'm seeing somebody, and I thought maybe we could grab dinner."

"Are you kidding me right now?"

My voice is harsh, and the women a few steps away from me, also waiting for their coffee, shoot me some looks. I must be talking louder than I realized.

"What? I thought you'd be happy to hear—"

"No, Dad," I hiss, heading toward the wall, from which I can still keep an eye on the espresso bar. "You asked me how things were going, and I told you 'not great'. So you take that as your cue to launch into telling me about some new chick you're dating? I can see you *really* care."

I lean my head against the exposed brick wall. My face is getting hot, my insides twisting. Of *course* this is how this conversation would go. When has my dad ever called to listen to me?

Answer: never. I'm the stupid one here.

"Aw, honey, I'm sorry. I didn't catch that. What's got you down?"

"It doesn't matter. Work stuff."

"The library?"

"Yes, the library. They're renovating, and I'm afraid it'll make getting historical landmark status a challenge. You know Mom always wanted—"

"Oh, Lydia." Dad's voice is as pitying as Mrs. Corey's face was. "That was a long time ago."

"Twenty years and two months, actually."

Dad clears his throat. "Honey, I know you miss your mom, and I know you love that library, but you've got to move on."

"Oh, right. Since *you* have done such a *great* job of doing that. You've moved on so well—right from one bar to the next!"

When Dad doesn't answer, my stomach sinks. I don't know where the fuck that just came from, but I'm too riled up to take it back. And anyway, it's not a lie. We've been through this before.

"Anyway," Dad says finally. His voice sounds tired over the blare of the far-off television. "I'd like you to meet Shelley sometime. She's wonderful. She teaches at the university, and she's—"

"I'm late for a meeting," I say, cutting him off. "Have a good day."

I jab at the phone screen to end the call, then stand with my eyes closed, head still resting against the wall. I know I should cut my dad some slack, be grateful that he's making at least *some* effort, after so many years of just... not caring. Or at least, not trying. But I can't. Not today.

When my phone buzzes again, I inhale sharply. Is he for real? You'd think a person would get the idea that their daughter doesn't want to talk to them when they—

Oh.

It's not Dad. It's Dylan again. When he decided he didn't want to be tied down three months ago, I deleted his number the same night. But of course I still recognize it. And although I haven't replied to any of his texts these last couple of days, I'm starting to wonder if I should. He hasn't said outright that he wants to get back together, but...

As the barista calls my name and I head to the counter to grab my coffee, I open the text and suck in a breath.

Jesus Christ, Dylan. That's... bold.

But his words barely have time to register, because no sooner do I swipe my coffee off the counter than I feel myself collide with something big and tall and solid, and my phone goes skittering to the floor.

three

WILL

Brewed Awakening is hopping this morning. It's a crisp, fall morning, and even the tables outside are packed with folks enjoying the weather. But I don't have time for that—I've got five minutes to get in, get out, and make it to the library before eight.

"Anything else this morning?" The chipper blonde behind the counter asks after I order my dark roast.

She looks up at me through mascaraed lashes and flashes me a smile. It's not just for the sake of customer service—she does this every time I'm in here. But she's too young, too nice. She doesn't know what kind of stock I come from.

Nah, this chick only *thinks* she wants a guy like me.

"That's all," I say, swiping my card. I stuff a couple bucks in the tip jar, just to be polite. It's not like I'm going to be stuffing anything else anywhere near her.

Glancing at my watch, I move to the far end of the counter. Four minutes until I'm late to my meeting, and I *hate* being late. Behind the flirty blonde at the counter, I see a barista set a fresh urn of coffee to brew.

"Goddamn," I mutter.

I know the blonde hears me because she shoots me an uncertain smile, but I don't apologize. Because, really. Drip coffee should *not* be taking this long.

I drum my fingers on the counter, wondering if the coffee's even worth it. I could dip out. If I hop in the truck now, it'll take me three minutes to get downtown, thirty seconds to park, forty-five seconds to sprint—

"Fuck!" I roar as something comes crashing into my chest.

Out of nowhere, a searing wetness hits me, scalding my bare forearms and scaring the living shit out of me. There's a clatter as something drops and goes skittering across the cafe floor. I look down at my shirt, where a dark stain is already soaking through the fabric. The line of customers to my right is frozen, and everyone in the whole damn place is craning their necks to see what the hell's going on.

"Well, that's just great," I hear a voice say. "There goes my coffee."

I snap my gaze up. I'd been gearing up to shoulder check the bastard who just drenched me with coffee, but that voice? It's definitely female.

And when my eyes land on the woman in question, who's got one luscious hip cocked to the side in a stance of defiance, my balls tighten despite myself—because she is *really* fucking female. And she's staring at me with a face that's absolutely livid. Which, honestly, is pretty damn rich, given the fact that *she* dumped her coffee on *me*.

That snaps me out of it.

"I'm sorry—*what*?" I bark out a harsh laugh, tugging at my stained, dripping shirt. "That's some apology you've got there."

She huffs out an exasperated breath, looks me up and down. She's clearly more upset that her coffee's gone than she is that she spilled it all over me.

"You know what? I *am* sorry—sorry you were standing so damn close to the counter. What were you *doing*?!"

"What do you mean what was *I* doing? I was standing here minding my own business!"

She scoffs and turns away, waving to the barista. As she gestures apologetically to her sopping cup, I can't help but notice the curve of her ass in her jeans. The way her hips are all pressed up against the counter. It's enough to set my balls to aching again, but I jerk my gaze away.

It takes a lot for me to lose control these days, and I'm sure as fuck not letting some smug-ass woman who can't even watch where she's going get to me. I'll rub one out when I get home tonight. It's always easier that way.

"Where's my phone?" The woman looks indignant, her eyes raking over me like she thinks I stole it or something.

I shrug. I'm still pissed about my coffee-stained t-shirt. I'm going to have to walk into this meeting looking a mess. Great way to start off a project I'm banking on for my career. Just superb.

The blond barista pours a stream of dark, silky coffee into a paper cup, snaps the lid on, and slides it to me across the counter with the flash of a sympathetic smile. As I move to take the cup from her, I accidentally kick something and stoop down to pick it up. I can feel Little Miss Smug's eyes on my back.

I flip the iPhone over in my hands and see the screen's lit up. I guess the non-apologizer was in the middle of a conversation when all hell broke loose. I know I shouldn't, but honestly, I barely realize I'm staring at the screen until I find myself reading the text that's in those little blue bubbles.

Can't stop thinking about how good you look sucking my cock. Choking on it. My hands tangled up in your hair, pulling til you scream.

I don't know if my eyes go wide, or if it's the little chuckle that escapes me that does it, but suddenly Miss Can't-Apologize lunges at me and snatches her phone out of my hand. I'm still a little shocked by what I just saw, but I can't bring myself to look at her yet because my dick's stiffening in my jeans and I just *know* I won't be able to avoid looking at her mouth and... imagining things.

I clear my throat.

Get your shit together, Will. You're in fucking public, and you're going to be *late*.

When I sense that Her Royal Smugness has turned back to the counter to take her second coffee from the barista, I pull it together enough to watch as she shoves her phone into her bag. The creamy skin of her neck is flushed pink. She knows I saw the text.

But the only thing she should be embarrassed about is the coffee. That text? Completely understandable.

This chick may need to learn how to take some responsibility, but I don't blame whoever sent it for wanting to pull that long, silky hair.

LYDIA

I am *mortified.*

Not only did I just dump a whole cup of hot coffee all over an *insanely* good looking man, but now he's also seen firsthand that Dylan wants to pull my hair while I suck his cock—and he's staring at me with an expression I can't quite read.

Make no mistake: It was *his* fault for standing too damn close to the counter. But holy shit, do I need to get out of here.

I snatch my second coffee from the barista. Twenty seconds ago, my gut reaction had been rage. First that stupid renovation, then Dad and his bullshit—and now *this.* But after that text, and the big, dark, wet stain on this guy's t-shirt, I'm so embarrassed my knees are shaking.

Too late, I remember my manners and shoot the guy an apologetic grimace before turning away from the counter. "Sorry about your shirt."

"No worries," he says with a snort. And then, as though

he just can't help himself, this asshole goes, "Guess spilled coffee isn't the only thing getting you hot and bothered today."

And that does it. Halfway to the cream and sugar, I freeze.

Drawing myself up to full height, I take a deep breath and turn around. If my knees were shaking a minute ago, now they're pulsing with adrenaline again. I don't make a habit of glossing over misogynistic comments the way it is, but I'm sure as *hell* not in the mood for it this morning.

"Oh, yeah?" I hiss, stalking toward him. I stop in front of him, so close I can feel the heat from his chest. "Well, maybe you should read that text again and heed the advice—and suck a *giant, fucking dick.*"

I know as the words leave my mouth that I'm overreacting, but I also can't help it. Too many things have gone wrong already this morning, and I don't have the strength to play nice.

He towers above me, and I force myself to look up at him. I can feel the eyes on us, the soft, uncertain laughs, but I won't back down. This guy picked the wrong person to mess with today.

"Jesus," the guy whistles. He runs a hand through his tousled dirty blond hair. There's a hint of a smile on his face, and it makes me even more livid.

"You think this is *funny?*" He clearly does—he doesn't need to tell me—and he's trying to hide it, like some kind of amused parent about to crack up at their toddler. "I don't know who you think you are, but—"

"*Jesus,*" the guy says again. He slides a hand under my

elbow and grips me tightly, steering me away from the counter. "Relax. Please, just—relax. We're good, okay?"

My cheeks burn. Not only am I embarrassed that a complete stranger is practically manhandling me in front of everyone in my favorite coffee shop, but I have the sudden realization of just how close this man *is*. How solid he is, how huge his palm is under my elbow. How good he smells.

Damn. I'm all over the place. I need to get a grip.

I shake myself loose from his grasp. I'm about to tell him that telling a woman to relax will *never* score you any points —and neither will physically moving her out the way—but then I look up into his face again, and I forget everything I was going to say. His eyes are the deepest blue I've ever seen, and they're fixed on mine.

"We're good," he repeats. "Okay? That… came out worse than I meant it to."

It seems like he's trying to apologize, but at this point I don't care. I'm too embarrassed, too annoyed at the world, and I've had *way* too little coffee to be dealing with this kind of shit. I'm also still stuck on this guy's eyes—and his perfectly chiseled jawline, which I'm pretty sure could cut ice if he'd let me test it out. Come to think of it, there are a few other things I'd like to test out with him.

But the guy's a jerk, and I'm not here for snarky remarks. I've got to get to the library. The stakeholder meeting is about to start, and if I want any hope in hell of getting them to hear my side of things, I'd better not be late.

"I don't have time for this," I say, pushing past him and out the door without a look behind. He's even more built than I thought, and the solid pushback of his shoulder as I pass him almost makes me wistful.

But it takes a lot for me to let my guard down. And now's not the time to start getting soft. I'm going to need every ounce of fight I have to take on whoever planned this restoration-turned-modernization project.

That library's my whole *childhood*. It's my safe place. And it needs to be preserved, exactly the way it's always been. Mom wanted it that way. It's the last connection I have to my mother, and if it's changed—if it becomes unrecognizable—I don't know how I'm going to hang on to her.

Which means I don't know how I'm going to hang on to *me*.

five

WILL

I'm the most embarrassed I've ever been in my entire fucking life when I leave Brewed Awakening. It's a good thing the air outside is cool because as I stomp to my truck and climb into the cab, I'm pretty sure I'm hyperventilating. That woman was *beautiful*—and I made a goddamn fool of myself.

Breathe in.

Keep it together, Will.

Breathe out.

You're a grown ass man.

I roll down the windows, letting the morning breeze drift through the cab as I drive. The cobblestones rumble beneath my tires, and I let the rhythm soothe me.

Then I bang the heel of my hand on the steering wheel. I am an *idiot*. A goddamn fucking idiot. When I picked up her phone and saw that text about sucking cock and pulling hair, I swear something in me turned feral. The way her jeans hugged her ass, the way she blushed when she knew that I'd seen, and her hair—*god*, her gorgeous silky hair. It was too much. I honestly thought I was going to have to jerk off in the restroom, just to make it out of there intact.

But even more than that, I feel like I violated her. She was clearly mortified—and then my stupid fucking mouth had to come out with *that* line, about being hot and bothered.

Way to make a woman feel good about herself, Will. You've really done your part in demonstrating what *not* pigs men are. Great—well done!

Fuck.

I'm pulling up to the library when my phone buzzes. I whip my pickup into a parking spot out front and flick through my phone's lock screen. It's a call from Ethan Wilde, one of the board members on the library project and the single wealthiest guy in Hawthorne Bay. When Ethan Wilde calls, I answer.

"This is Will."

"Will, hey," Ethan says. "Are you on the way?"

"Yeah, just pulled up."

"Great. Listen—before you get in here, I wanted to give you a heads up that we might get a little pushback during the meeting."

"Pushback?"

Ethan sighs. "Yeah, the assistant librarian has a bee in her bonnet about securing landmark status for the building —which isn't going to happen—and Eliza Corey from the Historical Society spilled the beans."

I frown. This is the first I'm hearing of this. "Spilled the beans?"

"Oh, we'd been trying to keep things under wraps,"

Ethan says. "Nancy, the head librarian, knew Lydia Chandler wouldn't go down without a fight, so we've kept things pretty mum regarding the design plans. And Lydia's not *wrong*. It *is* a gorgeous building. It's just that it'll be even better as an updated facility. It'll be good for the community."

"Right."

"Anyway, I'm sure things will be fine. I just wanted to let you know—in case she decides to show up and raise any issues. We *will* be going ahead with the plans we agreed on, so don't worry about that." He pauses a moment. "And you know, Holloway, if all goes well... I've got that coastline property I've been looking to rehabilitate."

I kill the engine and step down from the cab, slamming the truck door shut. "I may have heard something about that."

Ethan chuckles. "I figured. It'll be a big project, lots of historic architecture. I think you might be just the man, so long as I like your work on the library. But that's for another day. I'll see you in a few."

"Sure, no problem," I say. "See you."

Shoving my phone down the front pocket of my jeans, I stride up the sidewalk toward the towering, historic structure that is the Hawthorne Bay public library. As I jog up the concrete steps, I glance down at my watch. I'm officially three minutes late—but hey. Ethan didn't seem mad, and Ethan is who I care about.

Ethan Wilde could be what keeps a roof over my head and keeps Zeke's student loans paid. His project—this coastline one—could be the thing that pays off Mom's medical debt, which every month seems to bury me deeper and deeper. Ethan Wilde and his goddamn gorgeous project could be the thing that sets us up for life, and I will do whatever I have to do to get us there.

I'd rather die than let my siblings down. My old man already handled that one—hit the ball right out of the park—and I'm sure as shit not going to follow in his footsteps. So yeah, a beautiful woman who stands too close to me in a coffee shop and has curves like a fucking violin can get me hard, make me act a fool. But it's only a distraction. I've got to focus on what matters.

I need to screw my head on straight.

I do *not* need to be screwing anything else.

six

LYDIA

Lydia: OMG. Some asshole just bumped into me at Brewed Awakening and I dropped my phone and there was a text from Dylan on the screen and HE SAW IT.

Autumn: Saw what? Dylan's dick? Surprised it wasn't too small to see.

Lydia: Not a dick pic. But it may or may not have mentioned me choking on something…

Autumn: It's big enough to choke on?!

Lydia: Rude.

Autumn: 🔍

I'm still seething as I enter the library office, sipping my coffee and trying to regain my sense of composure. I power walked the whole way from the coffee shop, barely even aware that I was on the steps until I nearly tripped over them. My heart's still pounding, and the caffeine in this latte probably isn't helping.

I'm trying so hard not to think about what just happened at Brewed Awakening. My focus needs to be on this stakeholder meeting—not on some jacked douchebag who couldn't even watch where he was going.

The truth is, this meeting has been on the calendar for weeks. But, given that Nancy—my boss and the head librarian here in Hawthorne Bay—never uttered a single word about extensive modernization being included in the restoration plans, I wasn't very fussed about it. I guess I figured if whoever the board chose as architect had planned something that would upset me, Nancy would have said something.

Now I'm not so sure, and I'm really fucking antsy. If the board really *is* talking about making extensive changes, I'll have to get up and say my piece. Luckily, I've done my research. I think I can dissuade them, pull them over to my side.

At least I hope I can.

The board members are filing in now, along with the mayor and a couple of people I recognize as being on the city council. A few of them wave to me, and I nod back, flashing what I hope is a charming smile. Even Ethan Wilde, who's known around town for being the stereotypical brusque businessman ever since he lost his wife, shoots me a crisp nod. I've lived in Hawthorne Bay my entire life. These people know me. I read to their kids every Monday during story time. And they knew my mom, how much she loved this place when she used to work here. They know how important this historic building is to our town. I need to relax.

I take a long sip of my coffee. It's lukewarm by now, and the lack of sweetness is disappointing. Not only did that jerk at Brewed Awakening succeed in making my already shitty morning just a little worse, but he also ruined my latte by shaming me out of the place before I could add any sugar to it.

He really *was* a piece of work. Imagine. Picking up a total stranger's phone, reading their text message, and then proceeding to make a snarky-ass joke about it. Honestly, I should've tried to get a photo of him so I could out him on the internet for being a pretentious dick. I would've taken great joy in deleting that photo, too. Erasing his dumb face from my memory.

Ugh. I need to quit thinking about this dude. It's not like I'll ever have to see him again. Right now, what I need is to get my head in the game, figure out how I'm going to sweet talk whatever architect they've hired and get them to scale back a little on their plans. There's got to be a way for the library to get its glow up without compromising the—

"Hey, Ethan. How's it going?"

I hear the voice even before the face of the speaker registers, and it jolts me awake.

No. Fucking. Way.

Every shred of thought that might've been in my brain a second ago has gone straight out the window, because the guy who's standing in the front of the room shaking hands with the director of the board? It's Mr. Coffee Shop himself, in all his scruffy, muscled glory.

You have got to be *shitting* me.

"I've got the projector all set up for you," Ethan is saying. "So once you're settled and everyone's got a seat, I'll get us started. Looks like we're pretty much on time."

Projector? Once he's *settled*? What the fuck is he *doing* here?

"Good morning!" Nancy chirps as she slides into the seat next to me. She shoots me a chipper smile, then beams across the table at the rest of the board.

The guy from the coffee shop turns toward us with a polite smile, then stops, his eyes landing on me. His smile falters for a second, and I can tell he's struggling to piece together why the hell I'm here, but he recovers quickly.

"It's a lovely morning out there," he says, deep voice booming through the conference room. "Great weather."

I sniff. Nancy shoots me a glance, her brow furrowed.

"Lydia," she says, "Have you met Will Holloway yet? He's our architect."

An icy wave of horror floods through my bones. No. No way. This is *not* how this meeting was supposed to go. This can*not* be the architect. God fucking help me.

As the guy from the coffee shop fixes me with his blue-eyed gaze and gives me a polite nod, there's no way the expression on my face is anything but one of abject horror. But I snap my gaping mouth shut and try to pull it together.

"Um," I say, pasting on what I hope is a smile. "I think we've met once, yeah."

"I think you're right," Will says, something like a smirk playing on his lips. As he leans across the conference table and holds out a hand, I catch a whiff of his sweet, spicy cologne, and I hate it. He has no right to smell that good. "Either way—Will Holloway. Nice to officially meet you."

The last thing I want to do is shake this jerk's hand, but I've got no choice. Standing up from my seat, I pull my lips into a prim smile and return the handshake. His whole fucking hand about swallows mine.

Will's blue eyes are on me as I pull away. "Yeah," I say stiffly. "Nice to meet you, too."

"Alright," Ethan Wilde booms. He claps his hands together, and everyone settles into their seats. "Let's get started, shall we? By now, I'm sure you all know Will Holloway, and given that we're well on our way toward the pre-construction phase of the project, I'd imagine you're mostly familiar with the design plans, too."

A murmur of agreement ripples around the table, which I find a little concerning. Nancy's got her gaze fixed on Ethan, quite conveniently not looking at me.

"So following all that," Ethan continues," I'm happy to announce that the board has officially voted to approve the designs Will presented at the last meeting—with a few minor adjustments, which he'll walk you through in a few minutes."

Ethan turns to grin at the faces around the table, and it's only when the room erupts into polite applause that his words fully register. Did he just say the board has *approved* the designs? As in, past-tense, done-deal, that's-it *approved* whatever changes this Will character came up with?

If I thought I was frozen before when Will walked in, I'm sure as shit frozen now. Like, icicle status.

"I'm sorry," I hear myself blurt out. "You've already approved the designs?"

Every head in the room turns to look at me, including Ethan Wilde, who's not looking very pleased about being interrupted by the assistant librarian.

"We have," Ethan says, his voice curt. "The board voted last week."

"But I didn't..." I look helplessly at Nancy, but she's scratching at something on the table, still not looking at me. "I didn't know that was happening."

Ethan's smile is dangerously close to a sneer. "Well, you're not on the board, are you?"

The room's quiet. My face burns like he's slapped me, but I shake my head. He's right. I'm *not* on the board, which is exactly why I'm here at the stakeholder meeting—because as assistant librarian and a resident of Hawthorne Bay, I'm a damn stakeholder.

Will's eyes land on me, and I swallow hard. He's in on this shit. The man who just made a joke about me *sucking cock* is also the one who's going to gut the place that served as my only haven, and it makes me want to puke. Or throw my pencil at his stupid, chiseled jawline. He and Ethan Wilde can both suck ten dicks for all I care.

Ethan sits down at the table, his open laptop in front of him, and pulls up a presentation on the projector screen. He hands a clicker to Will. "Here you are. Take it away, Will."

Opening the sleek black binder he's placed on the table, Will smooths the pages and clicks his pen. He looks up at the screen, where a bulleted list has appeared.

"Alright. As you know, when the board first met to discuss the objectives of the project, our main aim was to preserve the integrity of the library while updating it to serve modern needs. To that end, our goals are threefold." Will counts off on his fingers. "Structural reinforcement and safety upgrades. Improved accessibility and space utilization. Expanded technological resources, meaning the new computer lab."

Everyone at the table nods as Will clicks through to the next slide. A large blueprint fills the screen, and Will gets up from his seat and strides over to it. He taps the screen with a large hand, and I crane my neck to get a look at the proposed layout. This is the first I'm seeing any of this.

"While the safety upgrades will include things like reinforcing the foundations, re-roofing, and updating the wiring and HVAC, you can see the main differences here in the floor plans are the wheelchair ramps and, of course, that new computer lab, which we'll actually be building on from scratch."

They're adding a whole new room onto the original structure? I frown, racking my brains to remember how much the area of a building can differ from its original floor plan to qualify for historical landmark status.

Suddenly, I feel my hand shoot up in the air like I'm a freaking high school student.

"Um..." Will says, nodding to me. "Lydia? You have a question?"

He's got this infuriating little smile on his face, and I see him share an amused glance with Ethan, who just shakes his head. I know I'm being a nuisance, but I don't care. This meeting's not only about these two assholes. It's about the *town*. It's about preserving *history*. And that's why I came to this meeting in the first place—to help them see just how important the historical authenticity of this building is to Hawthorne Bay.

"Yes. How many square feet is that?"

"Four hundred." Will's voice is steady as he meets my gaze across the room.

God, his eyes are blue. I look down at the table in front of me, knowing there must be pink creeping into my cheeks. "Is that... a lot?"

Will crosses his arms in front of his broad chest, the muscles of his biceps straining at the fabric of his t-shirt. With the way he's standing, I can't help but notice the slight curve in his jeans where his bulge is. I tear my eyes away from it. What the hell is *wrong* with me?

He cocks his head slightly, gives me a look that's somewhere between suspicion and amusement. Shit. If this guy—or *any*one in this room—just caught me checking out his bulge...

"It's substantial," he says, nodding.

For a second, I forget what I even asked. Because where my thoughts just were... let's just say his answer would have worked for that, too.

I pull myself together and clear my throat, looking around at the rest of the board. "Well, as you all know, Hawthorne Bay is an important town in Massachusetts state history. The Great Shipyard Fire of 1821 happened here, and every summer there's the Lantern Regatta commemorating the rescue efforts and rebuilding of the harbor. It's also a fact that the Hawthorne Bay Public Library is one of the oldest—if not *the* oldest—buildings in town.

"Over this past year, I got to thinking: Wouldn't it be great if we, as a town, and you, as a board, could secure historical landmark status for the building? It was something my mom always dreamed of—you know how much she loved this place. And aside from honoring the history of our town and our ancestors, it'd also serve us economically. I really think that with the right positioning—"

"I understand your concerns," Ethan says, his voice brusque. He clicks his pen against the table. "And we'll make sure the library's history is honored."

"Please," I say, looking steadily at both Ethan and Will. This is my final, last-ditch attempt to make them understand how important this is to me, and by god, I am not going to waste it. "I know I wasn't the only kid in Hawthorne Bay who spent days—literal *days*—basking in this library. Do you know what I used to do? It sounds silly now, but I used to pretend I was a princess, that the library was my castle. I'd curl up in a corner and read, all afternoon, and when it was closing time and the librarian would go around shutting off lights, I used to slide down that banister in the foyer and imagine I was—"

This time it's Nancy who cuts me off with a nervous laugh. She pats my arm, turning to look at me like I'm a little kid who just lost a soccer game. It's the same look Mrs. Corey gave me at our meeting this morning, and I fucking hate that Nancy's wearing it, too.

"Now, Lydia. I know you loved to come here as a child, but that's exactly *why* we need these additions. The library needs to fit the needs of our modern community."

"Well said," Ethan announces.

He turns back to Will, gesturing for him to continue, but Will hesitates, his gaze flitting sideways to see if I'll respond. But I don't. I don't have the energy to argue with these arrogant assholes. Not after they've made it so clear they're not interested in hearing me out.

The presentation continues, and Will's deep voice drones on. As he clicks through the slides, flicking through design renderings and pointing out features, I'm only vaguely aware of what he's saying. Under the table, I pull out my phone. If I let the details of this presentation sink in, I'm afraid I'm going to burst out crying. Or something.

Keeping my phone hidden under the table, I shoot off a text to Autumn, my best friend since college. I obviously didn't know her yet in second grade, but she knows all about how Mom used to bring me to the library after school and in the summer, and how I came on my own after Mom died because I had nowhere else to go. She knows how my last memory of Mom—last memory before it all went to shit, anyway—is here. Autumn knows what this place means to me.

LYDIA: So you know how the library's being restored or whatever?

AUTUMN: Yeah...

LYDIA: Well, it turns out they're basically gutting the place.

AUTUMN: NOOOO you're fucking kidding me!! Right??

LYDIA: I wish.

AUTUMN: So does that mean the landmark thing is out?

LYDIA: Ding ding. We have a winner.

AUTUMN: Wowwwww that's some bullshit right there

ME: Yep. Nancy obviously hid it from me. But the worst part is the architect is a total dick. I met him on my coffee run this morning before I knew it was him and he was the. biggest. asshole. And now he's sitting across from me. Talking about ripping up these awesome hardwood floors for fucking carpet.

AUTUMN: Well fuck him!

AUTUMN: Wait. Is he hot?

LYDIA: ...

AUTUMN: Ok, got it. He is.

LYDIA: He is not!

AUTUMN: Mmhm.

AUTUMN: Well, maybe you can bribe him...

I stop responding. Autumn is nuts. First off, I wouldn't stoop to that. Second, no matter how hot this Will Holloway is, there's no getting around the fact that the only reason he's here is to plow a bulldozer through my childhood. And *that* is an instant turn-off.

I can't wait for this meeting to be over.

I can't wait for Will Holloway to get the hell out of my sight.

seven

WILL

I'm trying so hard to concentrate during this presentation, but I can tell Lydia's texting beneath the table, and she's got this little smirk on her face that's making me crazy. There's no way she's not texting about me. Or—I feel my balls tighten as I sit back down in my chair and give Ethan the floor—maybe she's texting that guy. The one who wants to pull her hair while she sucks his cock.

Fuck. Any concentration I had just flew right out the window—because now I'm picturing what Lydia would look like, sliding underneath this table, unzipping my jeans, and drawing my cock into her pink little mouth while the rest of this meeting drones on. I wonder if she could even get the whole thing in. I wonder if Ethan would notice, if I could carry on talking about blueprints without my breath getting ragged while Lydia deep-throats me. Just thinking about it makes my dick twitch.

I saw Lydia eyeing my bulge earlier. She tried to act like she wasn't, but I'm not an idiot. Her eyes got all flustered and she blushed like hell—and how on earth I made it through my leg of the presentation without getting a hard-on is a damn miracle. I barely even remember anything she said after that, about how she spent a lot of time at the library as a kid. I did hear the bit about the banister, though. I'd like to see her slide down it now. In those jeans.

God. Focus, Will. You are a *professional*, for Christ's sake.

"Well, I think that'll do for today," Ethan is saying. He sits down, clasps his hands in front of him on the table, and looks around the conference room. "At some point we'll need to discuss plans for fundraising at the fall festival, but that can wait for the next meeting. So, regarding today's agenda, does anyone have any last questions? Concerns?"

My eyes flit to Lydia, even though I'm trying my damnedest not to imagine what her hair would feel like clenched in my fingers. I can see Ethan's looking at her too, almost like he's trying to dare her to start her bitching again. She doesn't take the bait.

Instead, it's Nancy who speaks. "I'd like to make a suggestion. Given Lydia's concerns about the more—uh—*modern* elements of the design, I thought it might be nice for Lydia to give Will a walkthrough of the building after the meeting." She turns to Lydia, pats her arm. "You know, highlight the historicity of the place? Come up with some ideas of how to preserve the historical charm of the structure?"

"With all due respect, Nancy," Ethan cuts in, "Will's experience renovating old buildings is fairly extensive. It's part of the reason we chose him."

I glance at Ethan, then at Lydia. Our eyes lock for a second before Nancy cuts in again.

"Of course, of course. It's just that Lydia's a Hawthorne Bay native with familial connections to the library, and I think her perspective could be valuable in making this place the best it can be."

Lydia scoffs. "I guess that's why you so obviously kept me out of the loop then, right?"

Oh, shit. Nancy's trying to smooth the situation over, but this is going *south*.

"You know what?" I say, jumping in with a broad smile. "I think that's a great idea. I can definitely stick around for a few minutes. It'll give me a chance to talk through some ideas about how to keep the story of the place alive and kicking."

Lydia stares at me like I just decided to rip my shirt off and go dancing around the room. It's clearly not what she expected, and I can tell by the way she narrows her eyes that she's more than a little suspicious, but I had to say *something*. It's been painful enough watching her get kicked around in this meeting. No way do I want to see her get herself fired.

"Fine," Lydia says. She gives me a clipped nod.

Everyone rises, and the board members all start to clear out. A few of the city council members stop to chat with me for a few minutes, invite me to participate in the booth the library's manning at the Hawthorne Bay fall festival to stir up interest from wealthy donors, and I play the part as best I can. I hate small talk, but when I'm the architect on a project and the hottest fucking investor in town is sitting there surveying me like a hawk, there's no way in hell I'm going to snub these people. Besides, I've got to stick around for this walkthrough or whatever it is.

"You ready?"

I look down to see Lydia standing next to me, examining her nails. She's got a binder tucked under her arm, and she's literally tapping her foot. This chick is unreal.

"Sure," I say. I toss my coffee cup in the trash. I hadn't thought my interactions with the woman at the coffee shop could get any more awkward, but here we are. "Let's do it."

As I follow Lydia out of the office and into the main room, I'm struck by how small she is. Her hand had been fucking tiny when I shook it, but now that I'm standing next to her when she's not screaming at me in a coffee shop, I feel like The freaking Hulk. I'm pretty sure I could pick her up one-handed—

Lydia stops suddenly, and I have to jump backward to keep from colliding with her. She spins around and studies me before striding over to one of the windows looking out on the street.

"Let's get something out of the way."

"Okay...?"

"I don't like you, and I'm not too dumb to see you don't like me, either."

"Wow. Shrewd observation skills you've got there."

"And you're clearly hilarious." Lydia rolls her eyes. "Anyway, you don't have to like me. I only ask that you keep an open mind about your plans for the building. That's what this is about. I know the board approved your designs, but..."

I cock my head at her. Her dark eyes are fixed on me, her expression serious. "Why do you care so much?"

"I told you. This place is a part of my childhood. A part of *me*, really."

"Huh." It's not a very concrete answer, but something tells me I've already seen too much of her personal life today to keep digging without pissing her off further.

"So, if you could just put your opinion of me aside for the next ten minutes and listen to what I have to say, that'd be great."

I shrug. I'm not going to change a design that Ethan Fucking Wilde has already approved for a woman I met an hour ago, but for her sake, I'll play along. "You got it."

"Good." She nods, then gestures to the row of windows in front of her. "These need to stay."

"Mm," I say, strolling lazily over to stand next to her and survey the windows that stretch across the wall. I point to the top row. "Eight-over-twelve sash windows. They do give it a New England feel."

"And the bay windows."

"I like those too," I say. "They let in a lot of light. But they're not historically accurate."

Lydia's eyes narrow. "Excuse me?"

"Exactly what I said. If you're trying to preserve the colonial features of the building, the bay windows aren't going to help. Judging by that multi-pane glazing, I'd say they were installed sometime in the mid-twentieth century."

I can tell I just knocked the wind out of Lydia, and honestly, it's pretty hard to hide the smirk I feel coming on. Leaning against the wall, I cross my legs and look up, gesturing toward the ceiling. "That dormer, though?" I whistle. "That's original. See how it's got those segmental, arched panes? That's representative of when the place was built, and I worked it into the designs. What else you got?"

"Okay, smart ass," Lydia snaps. She stalks to the other side of the room, and I follow her into the foyer, trying not to laugh. She's so small, but she's mad—and she's absolutely dripping venom. Her eyes land on the banister that spans from the main level down the half flight of stairs to the main entrance. "If you get rid of this banister, you're getting rid of a piece of history. I happen to know for a fact that this has been here since the building was constructed in—"

"1779," I finish. I wince, though, as I follow her gaze to the banister. "Unfortunately, if you'd paid attention to the presentation instead of texting under the table, you'd already know that it's being taken out."

Lydia's cheeks go pink. "Are you kidding me?"

"I'm very much not kidding, no. It's beautiful, but it doesn't fit the aesthetic we're going for. Would it help, though, if I told you I'm keeping the transom above the main entrance?"

Lydia stalks toward me. Her gaze is still hard, but the little wisps of hair that have fallen down to frame her face look so delicate, so soft. I actually feel a little bad for popping holes in all her hopes like this, especially after that story she shared about the banister. And with how close she's standing to me now, I find my mind straying back to that text. Goddammit.

"You're a real dick, you know that?"

"I've been told that before."

I need to get a handle on myself. I can feel my dick starting to harden again, and I think frantically of kittens. Of vomit. Of kittens vomiting. Anything to keep me from thinking about *her*, and the way she's got her dark eyes fixed on me. I can already tell she's going to be a thorn in my side until this project's done—for more reasons than one.

Lydia scoffs. "I guess someone told you you were funny, too."

"Never."

"Well, we're done here."

"Fantastic."

At this point, all I want is to get out of here. I've tried to be nice to Lydia, to go along with her weird obsession with this building and quell some of her fears, but it's not working. The only thing this walkthrough has succeeded in doing is making Lydia hate me more, which, alarmingly, I'm finding pretty attractive.

I fumble for the zipper on my jacket, tug it upwards.

The next thing I know, Lydia's shrieking in my ear, and Nancy's thundering into the foyer to see what the hell's going on. It takes me a minute to realize what Lydia's howling about, and when I do, I panic.

That long, silky hair of hers? That I've been walking around here fantasizing about? That that other guy wants to pull?

Yeah, it's caught in my zipper. And Lydia's face is right near my chest, and she's *pissed*.

"Holy shit," I stammer. "How did that even happen? Why was your hair even *near* my zipper?"

I have no clue what to do. Unzip? Or will that make it worse? Lydia's hair smells like vanilla and it's really fucking distracting, so I pull back slightly to get away from its heavenly softness.

"Stop moving!" Lydia demands. "Every time you move, it pulls!"

I can see that Nancy, although flustered by the awkwardness of it all, is trying her hardest not to burst into laughter. She leaves the room once more and comes back with a pair of scissors. She gives them a little snip in the air, which sends Lydia back to howling.

"Sorry, honey," Nancy says, her voice apologetic although she's stifling a smile. "Hold still."

She snips, setting us free, and pats Lydia on the back. She chuckles. "I guess you just didn't want Will to leave."

Lydia shoots her a death glare, and Nancy leaves the foyer, scissors in hand, shoulders shaking as she enters the office. I zip my jacket for real this time. Lydia's blushing furiously, and I'm still fighting my hard-on. Beautiful as she is, she's coming across as childish. I've had one too many weird encounters with this woman for a single morning, and I'm out.

"Listen," I say to her as she examines the ends of her hair. "Don't take this the wrong way, but... all our other issues aside, you need to move on. Let the past go. It's not a good look for you."

And with that, I walk out, leaving her standing in the foyer, fuming. It's only when I get to my truck and unzip my jacket again that the snipped ends of Lydia's hair fall from the teeth of the zipper and into my lap. I slide them into my jacket pocket—I can't help it, they smell so fucking good— and drive.

eight

LYDIA

Dylan: Been thinking about you. About your mouth. I miss you.

Lydia: Yeah?

Dylan: Yeah. Wanna come over?

Lydia: You're laying it on kind of thick.

Dylan: I am kind of thick.

Lydia: Good night, Dylan.

I haven't had to see Will Holloway since the stakeholder meeting on Monday, which is a huge fucking relief, given that our last interaction had me with my hair in his damn zipper. After the incident with the coffee, the embarrassment of the meeting, and that absolute joke of a walkthrough, I really didn't need any other shit to go down between us. It didn't help that Nancy was shaking with laughter for the rest of the afternoon.

But I'm not thinking about that today. It's a glorious Saturday morning, and Autumn and I have made our way down to the harbor for the weekend Farmers Market. It's sunny, but the air is chilly enough for a sweater, especially with the breeze coming off the sea. It's the kind of crisp fall morning I live for here in Hawthorne Bay.

Autumn jabs me in the ribs. "Are those caramel apples?"

I look where she's pointing. Sure enough, rows of golden apples stuck with popsicle sticks cover a nearby table. "Looks like it. You want one?"

"In a minute." Autumn's already veering off toward a different table, where rows of glass jars filled with various kinds of herbs and dried fruits sit lined up. My arm's linked with hers, and I'm yanked along behind her. "I'm pretty sure these are cocktails you can make at home."

She lifts up one of the glass jars, inspecting the contents. Dried lime rind, several sprigs of fresh mint, a scattering of bright pink flower petals. "It's a mojito in a jar! You only have to add rum."

Her enthusiasm makes me chuckle. "Yeah, since we all have rum sitting around at home."

"Lydia, babe. Not everyone's as square as you are." Autumn feigns a scoff and shoots me a playful wink. "Anyway, drinking at home is boring. If I want a cocktail, I'm heading to the bar."

I shake my head, laughing. This is what I love about Autumn. She may have married crazy rich, but she's not too above the rest of us to put on a mini skirt and strut her way into a dive bar. She'll have every head there turning, too.

"Hey."

My heart jumps into my throat as a deep voice startles me out of my thoughts and I catch a whiff of spicy, sweet cologne. You have got to be *kidding* me.

"Uh, hi," I stammer, turning around to see exactly who I thought I would. "What are you doing here?"

Will laughs, blue eyes crinkling. The top button of his red flannel shirt is undone, and I catch a glimpse of chest hair as he brushes his tousled hair out of his eyes. He looks even better than I remember. I hate it. "You do know I live in Hawthorne Bay, right?"

"Who're you?" Autumn asks before I can answer, looking Will up and down. Her eyes narrow for a second, and then an absolutely wicked grin spreads across her face. "Oh, you must be the architect."

Will's eyes flit to mine, and I feel my face grow hot. I unlink my arm from Autumn's and give her a sharp jab in the ribs with my elbow. Will's mouth twitches.

He reaches out to shake Autumn's hand. "Will Holloway. And yes, I do happen to be an architect."

Just then, a tall, lanky guy with white-blond hair strides up to Will and punches him on the shoulder. "Yo. You are one lucky bastard, not having to see that gnarly dude with the missing nose hanging out by the Jack-o-lantern booth. Every time I look over there I—" The guy stops, seeing Autumn and me, and a slow, dazzling smile creeps almost imperceptibly onto his face. He's got the same chiseled jawline as Will, but there's something about this guy that's way more smooth. "Hey, ladies."

Curious, I glance toward the booth selling freshly carved Jack-o-lanterns. There are quite a few people milling around near it, none of them with missing noses. I have no clue what this scarily suave kid is talking about, but I'm sure as hell not going to ask.

Will just snorts. "Don't you ever turn that charming shit off?"

The guy doesn't take his eyes off me and Autumn. "Not a chance."

"Well, at least you're your own red flag," Will says, giving the younger, lanky guy a playful shove. He looks at Autumn and me, his eyes almost apologetic. "My brother, Zeke, folks."

"Red flag is right," Autumn mutters, but she looks more amused than anything. Her eyes snap back to Will's. "You've got your hands full."

"You're telling me. He's supposed to be getting a job, but, funny story, he hasn't gotten any interviews." Will casts an irritated look at his brother.

"Don't blame me, man," Zeke says, shrugging. "You're the one who helped me write my resume. If you don't know how to write a resume that doesn't suck, you should just own up."

Will just grunts in reply.

"Yeah, whatever," Autumn says, waving a hand. "Anyway. Will. You're the one redoing the library?"

Will nods. "It's going to be a beautiful building."

"It already *is* a beautiful building," I snap.

"Also true."

Suddenly, Will's brother whistles. He steps away from us to gaze across the harbor, shielding his eyes with a smooth, tan hand. "Damn. Now *that* is one beautiful piece of ass."

Will groans, looking to Autumn and me like we're going to give him some kind of sympathy. I follow Zeke's gaze. I'm grossed out by his vulgar objectification, but I'm also wondering what kind of woman would draw such an immediate reaction from this guy who's clearly used to getting whatever female attention he wants.

But as soon as I look, I wish I hadn't. There's only one couple on the other side of the harbor, and when my gaze lands on them, my stomach plummets.

Because there's Dylan. And he's got his arm around some blond, Barbie-looking bombshell.

Apparently, I didn't respond to his text fast enough.

nine

WILL

"Dude. You need to chill," I hiss, giving Zeke a sharp elbow to the ribs as Lydia and Autumn look to see who it is my brother so crassly pointed out. Shoving him out of earshot, I stab my finger into his chest. "First off, don't talk about women that way. Second, you're embarrassing me."

"Oh, boo hoo." Zeke rolls his eyes. "I'm *obviously* trying to make the redhead jealous. Don't you have *any* game, bro?"

The redhead? As in… Lydia's friend, Autumn?

"That woman is absolutely not jealous. If anything, she's revolted."

Zeke grins. "You just wait, bro. And remember—I call dibs. Don't even *think* about making a move on her."

I glance toward Lydia. She and Autumn are talking in hushed whispers, and there's something on her face that looks absolutely… devastated. Her gaze keeps going back to the couple on the other side of the harbor.

Zeke narrows his eyes at me. "What's that look for? Did you fuck her already?"

"No, I did not," I snap. "We're not *all* sex crazed, you know. I've never seen her before in my life. But if she's Lydia's friend, I can tell you right now that she is *not* trying to get it on with some douchey twenty-two-year-old."

A smirk creeps over my brother's face. "Ohhh. Lydia. I see, you fucked the *brunette*."

"Knock it off," I growl. This kid is really starting to annoy me. "I have *not* fucked the brunette, and you'd better keep your goddamn voice down if you want a roof over your lazy head."

"Oh? Why's that?"

"Because she's the assistant librarian at the Hawthorne Bay public library—for which I am currently in charge of renovations."

Zeke pushes a slim hand backward through his hair, making it stand on end. He smooths it down again. "A librarian, huh? You like her."

"As a matter of fact, she's a pain in my ass—even more than you, if you can believe that."

"Boo," Zeke says. He cranes his neck to look at Lydia and Autumn again. "Looks like the redhead's got a huge ol' rock on her left hand. I'm not messing around with that."

I snort. "I'd say that's probably for the best."

"And I'd say your brunette knows the guy with that blond chick over there. Love how they picked the missing nose guy to stand next to."

Zeke juts his chin toward the couple, and I whip my head around again.

Thankfully, I can't see whatever ghost with the missing nose Zeke keeps talking about. But I *can* see that Lydia has gone up to the flesh and blood guy, who's dressed in a tight-fitting polo and has so much gel in his hair I can see it glimmering from where I'm standing. I can't hear anything Lydia is saying, but when she goes in for a hug, the guy goes all loose, slides one half-assed arm around her back. The woman he's with—the blond one Zeke called a piece of ass—looks genuinely confused, but Autumn's staring at Polo Guy like he's the scum of the earth.

I see Lydia give a nervous laugh, touch the guy's arm. He flinches away, and her face falters. But the next second, her too-wide smile is back, and she's waving goodbye to him, tugging Autumn after her into the crowd. It's only when they reach a table covered with caramel apples that she lets the pasted-on grin slide. From across the way, Polo Guy shoots her this awful, pitying smile and places his hand on the small of the blond chick's back as they head to a different booth.

"That dude is absolutely stringing your girl along," Zeke remarks.

"She's not my girl."

From the looks of things, Zeke's not wrong. I have no clue what the context of that little meet-up just was, but frankly, it's not my business. I've got too much on my plate right now to go adding other people's drama to the mix.

"Whatever," Zeke says. He's already striding toward the caramel apple booth, where Autumn's standing with one hip jutting out, surveying the spread. There's no telling what this kid's going to say next, so I sigh and follow him. I've turned into his walking damage control.

Lydia glances back at the same moment Zeke and I approach the table. She catches my eye, cocking her head at me. "Are you... following us?"

"Maybe," Zeke says with a wink. He quirks an eyebrow. "Do you want us to be?"

Lydia flicks a hand at him, but there's laughter in her voice when she says, "You're pretty full of yourself, kid."

Zeke leans against the table, and his eyes flit to Autumn's. "And for good reason."

"Okay," I cut in, handing the high school kid a five-dollar bill as he passes Zeke a caramel apple. Whatever happened to *the redhead's got a rock on her finger*? "We get it, Zeke. If flirting were a viable career, you'd be a fucking billionaire."

Lydia's quiet, studying Zeke. "You said you're looking for a job, yeah?"

"Mmhm." Zeke takes a bite of the apple, licking his lips as he crunches for a moment. "I mean, in theory. Gotta do something about my resume. Will doesn't know what he's—"

"I'll take a look at it."

"Huh?"

"I'll take a look at your resume," Lydia repeats. She digs around in her bag for a second, then jots something down on a memo pad and hands it to Zeke. "That's my email. Send me what you've got, and we'll go from there. I know if it were me I'd want to get out from under The Hulk's roof as soon as possible."

"Daaamn," Zeke says through a mouthful of caramel. He's looking at Lydia in awe. "Right on. You're awesome."

Lydia shoots me a snide glance, and I can't tell if she's

reveling in her Hulk comment or trying to rub it in that, for this moment at least, my little brother seems to prefer her to me. Both, probably. The way she looks at me before turning to choose a caramel apple from the spread on the table is infuriating. What's she trying to do? Show me up in the skill of useless document writing? Prove my own brother thinks I'm incompetent?

Still, I'd be lying if I said I'm not a *little* impressed with the way she handled Zeke just now. How she snapped him out of his antics and, not only that, managed to get an actual answer out of him? Dang. I'm also a little—wow, it's hard to admit—*touched* that she'd offer her time and expertise to help this jerk of a kid start getting his shit together.

Shoving Zeke away from the table, I slip a ten-dollar bill to the kid working the booth and tip my head toward Autumn and Lydia, who are still deciding whether they want pecans or sprinkles. The kid flashes me a grin to show he understands, and I turn and leave, falling into step beside my brother.

Lydia intrigues me. Her jabs at me are expected, but I'm not sure what to make of her generosity to my brother, who she just met, or that shattered look she got when she saw that couple on the dock. There's clearly a story there that I'm not privy to, but remembering the way her shoulders fell when that guy would barely hug her back... I could've punched him.

She may hate me, but she doesn't deserve that kind of shit. And if a caramel apple on a stick is going to make her day a little better after putting up with a douche like that? Hell, I'm there.

LYDIA

Dad: Hey. Want to come have dinner with
Shelley and me th s weekend?

Lydia: Sorry, I've got plans.

Dad: Next weeker d?

Lydia: I'll have to see.

Dad: Give me a chance here, Lydia. I'm
really trying.

Lydia: Sorry, Dad. I've got a lot going on.

Over the course of the next few days, Will's team is in and out of the library. From what I can tell, it's just a couple of engineers and some kind of interior designer, and they're still mapping things out, so they've stayed largely out of my way so far. Which I'm glad of—because with every ladder that comes through the door and every tape measure I hear snapping shut, I'm reminded of what they're in here to do.

I haven't seen Will Holloway himself—except in passing—since Saturday, when he showed up at the Farmers Market with that sleazy yet weirdly charming brother of his and thought he'd score some quick points by paying for a couple of caramel apples. Autumn seemed to approve and wouldn't shut up about him, but I'm pretty sure Will must've seen how Dylan blew me off for that Barbie hanging on his arm and took pity on me. Had to play the hero, absolve himself of the role he's playing in wrecking the library by paying me off.

Well, fuck him. He can't even write a good resume. I don't need his pity—I've got *that* part down.

I don't know how I could've thought Dylan's brazen texts last week meant he actually wanted something with me. I was stupid. Like *duh*, Lydia. A guy doesn't dump you only to try to win you back four months later via X-rated texts. And when he comes to the Farmers Market with a bombshell on his arm? Even *if* she was his "friend" like he said she was, he couldn't even hug me.

Yeah. Stupid. Stupid and pitiful.

But I'm trying not to think about it. I'm shelving books in the mystery section this afternoon, and since Nancy's already gone home for the day, it's just me and the books. The solitude is soothing. Aside from the faint hum of male voices somewhere in the building, the only sounds in the room are the crackle of the plastic dust covers and the squeak of my cart as I wheel it between the aisles. This place... it's still how I remember it.

Sliding an Agatha Christie novel onto the shelf next to its counterparts, I let my gaze wander the room. A darkening pink-orange sky is visible through the panes in the dormer, and fading, golden sunlight streams in through the bay windows, flooding the reading nook a few aisles away. My throat feels suddenly tight. That reading nook—particularly the armchair there, now bathed in shimmering golden hour light—was Mom's and my spot.

After her first round of chemo, when Mom couldn't get around very well anymore but still wanted to leave the house, we'd come here to read together. We'd squeeze into the armchair, and Mom would read aloud to me, her voice soft and steady as we escaped together into another world—one where Mom didn't hurt, where Dad wasn't sad, and where I wasn't terrified of being alone. Sometimes other kids would come, plopping casually down next to us or hanging over the back of the chair, and Mom would read to them, too. We all loved her voice, the way she did the characters and paced her reading to match the action. All the way up until almost the end, when she started having a hard time forming words correctly, Mom always had a crowd of kids hanging around, asking sheepishly for a story.

And after she was gone...

Fuck.

After she was gone, I came here by myself. I did whatever I could to get out of my dark, lonely house, to be wherever I thought any sparks of Mom's energy might still be lingering.

I knew it was silly, but I didn't care. I was desperate. I used to climb up into that armchair, which now felt so vast, so empty, and pretend Mom was sitting next to me, that I could still feel her warmth and the weight of her arm around me. I guess I thought I could keep her from slipping away completely—I don't know. It's hard to say what goes through the mind of a ten-year-old, even when that ten-year-old is you.

I'm jerked out of my thoughts when Will comes striding into the fiction section, a ladder over his shoulder and his sweaty t-shirt stuck to his chest. The outline of his pecs is visible through the darkened gray of his shirt, and I tear my gaze away to concentrate on the cart that's piled with Agatha Christie hardbacks. I've got work to do. I guess I should be grateful he tore me out of my memories.

"Hey."

It's the only word he says as he sets the ladder down with a clang. I flit my gaze to his and nod. Using the bottom edge of his t-shirt, he wipes the sweat from his brow, and I catch a glimpse of his well-defined stomach glistening beneath. Holy shit, this guy is ripped.

But I don't let my gaze linger. I don't think Will's sense of self-importance can get any more inflated, but I'd rather not find out.

"What do you need?" I ask, not looking up from my cart.

"Just taking some measurements vents."

"Well, you'll have to wait. I'm working."

Will blows out his breath. "Seriously? It'll take ten minutes. The rest of my guys already went home."

"Seriously," I say, finally looking up at him. "I don't know what part of 'I'm working' you're not getting, but I'm re-shelving. I'll let you know when I'm done."

"Jesus." Will shakes his head and looks away, an irritated half-smile flashing across his face, like he can't believe he has to work with me. "Okay, how about this? I've got to get behind this bookcase to check the wall thickness. You hold off for a sec while I do that, and then I'll do the rest after you leave tonight. You won't have to see my face, and I won't have to hear you bitch at me."

I scowl at him, but I want him out of my hair and this feels like the quickest way. "Fine. Make it quick."

Will only grunts in reply. As I wheel my cart past him, I catch the tiniest whiff of his cologne. It's mixed with sweat, but it's still delicious, and I hate it. I also hate that I'm still fighting the urge to stare at the way his dampened t-shirt clings to his solid chest.

"Stand over there," he instructs, pointing to the far wall. "These bitches are heavy, and I'd rather not have to deal with any crushed limbs."

"How kind of you." I'm not about to follow his pointing finger, but I move toward the adjacent wall where he set down the ladder, and he seems satisfied.

Leaning against the wall, I watch as Will pushes one of the heavy bookcases out from the wall. His shoulders strain beneath his t-shirt, biceps rippling as he grimaces with the effort. His arms look absolutely massive. Too bad he's such a massive dick. And apparently also *has* a massive dick.

God. I've been listening to Autumn too much, who keeps

telling me the fastest way to getting these blueprints changed is to get *under* the architect. I need to get a handle on myself.

Having lifted the far end of the book case, Will's now on the other side of it, coming to push the other end toward the center of the room. I can hear him cursing under his breath.

"You good?" I ask, in spite of myself. It's not like there's much I can do to help if he isn't. These bookcases are insanely heavy, and a little part of me is impressed he's able to move them around by himself.

"Yeah," he grunts. Although he's not far from me, he's still on the other side of the bookcase, so I can only hear his voice through the shelves. "I think there's a nail or something in the floorboards, though. It's caught on something."

I sigh loudly. "Want me to go get one of the other guys you have traipsing through here? I don't have all day."

"I told you. They went home."

I can't see his face, but I see the bookcase wobble. He must still be trying to get it over the catch in the floor. Knowing he can't see me, I roll my eyes. Men. Always have to do everything themselves.

Suddenly, the nearby end of the bookcase—the one Will's directly behind—jumps a foot in the air and the top of it teeters wildly. Books start avalanching down, and it takes a second before I can even tell what's happening, they're falling off the shelf so fast. Barely thinking, I throw myself backward, crashing into something behind me.

And then everything happens so quickly it's a blur. I must've crashed into the ladder, because suddenly, I turn to see it towering above me, wobbling dangerously and then falling toward me. I freeze. My whole body's cold. But then Will shoots out from behind the bookcase and hurls himself at me, his huge arms coming on either side of me to catch the ladder before it crashes onto my head. I'm face to face with his chest, and it's even more solid up close than it looks from afar.

Still frozen from shock, I realize I'm barely breathing. As Will strains to right the ladder, the hem of his shirt slides up, revealing two delicious lines that slope down into his jeans and make my breath hitch even more.

It's also hard not to notice the curve of his bulge, which is now about an inch away from me. It looks... substantial. Like he said.

Will shoves the ladder back against the wall, and it lands with a clang. He stands looking at it for a moment, panting, and then, as though deciding better, strides past me to pick it up again. Carefully, he maneuvers it away from me and lays it down on the ground. Then he turns back to me and glares.

"I thought I told you to stand by the far wall."

Seriously? No 'are you okay'? No sign of concern, no nothing? I don't care how many caramel apples he buys me—this guy is a piece of work.

"Okay?" I snap, feeling my anger rise. "And? *You* shouldn't have leaned the ladder against the wall like that!"

"Well, it wouldn't have mattered if you'd just done what I asked you to!" His voice is a growl.

Did he just save me from getting crushed by a ladder? Sure. But to blame *me* for his mistake? Get real. This time I let him see me roll my eyes. And then I walk right up to him—so close we're almost touching—and look up into his face, meeting his glare with one of my own.

"So, what?" I say, pressing a finger into his solid chest. "You're not the boss of me."

As soon as the words leave my mouth, I know how childish they sound. But I don't care. Because Will Holloway has royally pissed me off, and I'm sick of being polite.

eleven

WILL

Lydia's standing in front of me, her head tipped back so she can see all the way up to glare at me, and she's got her finger poked into my chest. If she didn't look so goddamn scary, I might be tempted to think about the way her breasts are pressed up ever so slightly against me.

Scratch that. I *am* tempted. More than tempted. There's something about the way she's snarling at me that makes me want to grab her breasts and squeeze. Drag my teeth down her neck, slide that collar down her creamy fucking shoulder and—

"You think you're some kind of hero, huh?"

My brain comes to a screeching halt. I look back at her, confused. I *did* just save her from having a pile of metal come straight down on her head—which honestly, I think I deserve some thanks for—but I sure didn't say anything about being a hero.

"I have no clue what you're even talking about," I huff out.

"Oh, quit playing dumb," she all but spits. She drops her hand from my chest. "You trot your little brother out, showing off how *kind-hearted* you are in taking him in, and then you buy my friend and me a couple of fucking caramel apples—like we can't buy them ourselves! You thought you really did something there, didn't you? Wow, Will Holloway, what a *nice* guy, what a—"

"Well, excuse the *fuck* out of me," I retort. "I was trying to do something nice. I saw how that gelled up, prep school dickwad blew you off, and I wanted to make your day better. Pardon me for wanting to fucking help!"

"Oh, please. You're no better than he is," Lydia says, her voice dripping with spite. "You're just another self-centered prick."

Her words hit like a brick, straight to the face. She's breathing hard, like she's waiting to see what I'll say. Maybe I *am* a selfish prick. My dad definitely was, walking out on us like that. Thinking that, because he paid child support, it somehow absolved him of what he did to us. And here I am, buying caramel apples and catching falling ladders like it makes up for what I'm doing to the building this woman so obviously cares about—even if I don't get why she does.

Maybe she's right.

I stare at her for a moment. She's so fucking beautiful, her dark eyes all narrowed like that, glinting with anger in the golden afternoon light that streams through the window above us. I can feel the heat from her body, and as I stare at her, her eyes fixed back on mine, I feel my dick hardening in my pants. It's so close to her stomach. Only a zipper and a strip of denim between my cock and her smooth, creamy skin.

As I take a half step toward her, closing the tiny gap between us, Lydia's still glaring up at me. We're so close our bodies are touching now, and my cock is fully hard—there's no way she doesn't feel it. But she doesn't move. Doesn't back away.

Suddenly, my hands are around her ass, and I'm pulling her into me so she can feel every inch of my length. Feel how hungry I am for her. How much she's making me crazy. I'm still waiting for her to pull away—to show some sign that this isn't what she wants—but she's standing stock still, her palms on my chest.

Running my hands down the curve of her hips, I lean down and brush my lips against her ear. Give her ass a gentle squeeze.

"I may be a selfish prick," I say into Lydia's ear. "But I guarantee you I'm better than he is."

"Oh, yeah?" She looks up at me. There's a challenge in her eyes behind the anger. "Prove it."

And then something erupts.

In a split second, I've lifted her off the ground and she's wrapping her legs around me, our mouths are crashing together like we're crazed, starving fools. Which maybe we are—starving *and* fools. Because it's been a while, and Lydia's ass in my palms and her tongue in my mouth is delicious.

It's also crazy. This woman hates me.

But I don't care. Right now, I only care that Lydia's mouth

is soft and full, that she's running her tongue over my bottom lip as I hike up her skirt and knead her ass beneath my palms. I slip my tongue between her lips, and she grinds against me, whimpering, wrapping her legs tighter. It's impossible not to think about what's there between them, about what she's rubbing against me so desperately, when there's only a strip of lacy fabric covering it. A *damp* strip of fabric.

My cock is rock hard, and it's all I can do not to unzip my fly and let my entire length spring free. But that wasn't part of the challenge. I said I was better than that hair-pulling, frat boy motherfucker, and Lydia asked me to prove it. Although taking out my dick and wrapping her fingers around it sounds divine right now, it also screams 'selfish prick'.

And we can't have that.

Still gripping Lydia by the ass, I carry her to the far side of the room, setting her back gently against a spot of wall between the bookcases. She's pinned between the wall and me, her ankles hooked behind my back. I pull away from Lydia's mouth for a moment, tracing kisses down the length of her collarbone, my cock still straining at my jeans.

Thank god there's nobody else here.

Using my hip to pin her to the wall, I shift my weight just enough to slide one hand out from under her. I bring my eyes to hers, searching there for any sign of hesitation as my fingers trace along her inner thighs. Her eyes are wide, but she holds my gaze. Even as my fingertips find the lace of her panties, dipping ever so slightly beneath the elastic and meeting soft, soft skin, she doesn't break my stare. Instead, she nods.

That nod is all I need. Pulling her skirt up so it's completely around her waist now, I tug her panties to the side. Although her eyes are still on mine, I can't help but look down to admire the view. Her slick, pink cunt is on full display, legs still spread on either side of me. I swipe my finger gently down the middle of her core and feel her shudder. Lydia is *dripping*.

I bring my eyes back to hers and hold her gaze as I lick clean the finger that just grazed her. Then, with the very tip of my finger, I begin tracing circles around her clit, keeping my rhythm steady even as she straight out the gate tries to shift her hips to get me to touch her clit itself.

I move my mouth once again to her ear. "Do I still need to prove it?"

"Yes," she breathes. "Fuck yes."

"Then let me do my job," I growl.

Her only answer is a throaty groan as she lets her head fall back against the wall. But her hips still, and I feel her loosen against me. My fingers are slick with her wetness, and as I continue my circles around her swollen bud, it's all I can do to keep it together.

And the way Lydia's starting to writhe again, I can tell she's sufficiently teased. I brush my thumb over her clit, and she bucks her hips against me. I stop my circling.

"Will," she breathes. Her voice is mangled with want.

"Mm?" I'm enjoying baiting her. Bringing her to the edge.

"Aren't you going to do your job?"

I let out a low chuckle. "You are *impatient*, Ms. Chandler—"

And then her lips are on mine and I'm cut off. She's pulling my head toward hers, and is kissing me so savagely I'm honestly lost for a moment. Her lips taste so fucking good, and the way she's got her hands on the back of my head, fingers tangled in my hair, is downright sinful. There's no way I can say no to that. Not when she's asking so nicely.

Breaking away from the kiss, I graze her earlobe with my teeth. "Message received."

Then, yanking her panties to the side again, I slip one finger into her pussy, relishing the way she melts completely into me at that touch alone. She's so fucking wet it takes only a couple of slides in and out before I add a second finger, plunging in and out of her as I work her clit with my thumb. She's writhing under me, giving these little moans of pleasure right in my ear, but she lets me take the wheel.

All I want is to drop down to my knees and taste her, but my left hip is the only thing keeping her against the wall. And by now, Lydia's breaths are so short and fast, her whimpering so insistent, that I think she might actually kill me if I stop what I'm doing.

So I keep on, plunging in and out, stroking her inner wall and trying not to let how tight she is distract me. My cock is straining at my jeans, basically begging me to be let loose, but it can wait. I already know I'm going to fuck my hand tonight while thinking of this woman.

Suddenly, Lydia gives a long, low moan, her fingers tangling tighter in my hair, and absolutely shatters. Her pussy clenches around my fingers, spasming with pleasure, but I keep my thumb on her clit while we ride out the wave together. I'm horny as all hell, but I'm also high on Lydia's pleasure. Turns out making someone who hates you come hard is an interesting kind of vindication.

Lydia drops her head back against the wall, and I can't resist rubbing the scruff of my beard against the smooth skin of her neck before giving a playful bite to her ear lobe.

"Told you it'd be good." I slide my fingers out of her pussy and suck them clean.

Lydia draws in a deep, shuddery breath. Her eyes flutter open, and we stare at each other. Now that the heat of the moment has broken, neither of us knows what to do. Some invisible line has been crossed, and I can tell that both our minds are racing, trying to figure out how the fuck to scramble back over it. I don't think we can.

Gently, I lower Lydia to the floor, tugging her skirt back down around her ample hips. My cock's still throbbing in my jeans, but I'm doing my best to ignore it. I hope she can't see it.

Lydia re-centers her skirt around her waist. When she finally looks up at me, it's like her face is made of stone—like she's put on this mask that she doesn't want me to see behind.

"You were right," she says simply. "I stand corrected."

That makes me grin. "Did I just hear you concede defeat?"

She tosses her hair, then nudges me aside so she can walk toward the door. "Don't push your luck, Holloway. You either heard me or you didn't."

"Oh, I heard you, beautiful," I say, following behind her.

"It's a damn good thing Nancy left early, because this whole *building* would've heard—"

"Stop it," Lydia hisses. "And don't call me that."

She comes up behind me, trying to shove me through the door and out into the foyer. I'm too big for her, though, and her slender little palms on my back don't move me an inch. I flash a grin over my shoulder. She's got me feeling cocky now, knowing I did my job well.

"This doesn't change anything," she says. Her cinnamon eyes narrow as she glares at me. "So you can make me come —so what? You're still a self-centered asshole who cares more about how much money he'll make than he does about what another person—or community—needs."

Her words are like a slap in the face. Because I'm pretty sure she's right. When it comes down to it, that's exactly what I'm doing. It's not just for me, though—right? It's for Zeke, too. And Benji and Phoebe. The opportunity that lies on the other side of this library project could change our fucking lives. Still, I don't like knowing *I'm* the one crushing Lydia's dream. It makes me feel like shit.

"Fine," I say coolly. "I won't offer again."

"Good. It's unprofessional."

Lydia closes the door in my face and I'm left standing out in the foyer. The last rays of the afternoon sun seep golden through the windows, casting long shadows across the hardwood floor. It really is a shame we're planning to be getting rid of it—it's beautiful. And carries the presence of thousands of souls who've walked across it over the past two hundred years.

Suddenly, a rush of cold, like someone's icy breath, sweeps across my neck. I freeze.

What the *fuck*?

I know that feeling—and I can't be feeling it. There's no *way*. My mind must be going off. I shut that ghost shit down forever ago, have spent way more fucking hours meditating than I ever thought I would in my *life*—all to make sure that energetic wall I managed to build when I was 18 never gives an inch. And it works—usually. I keep those spirits *out*. They can knock sometimes, but there's no way they can get in.

I never asked for whatever this ability is, and it's only ever brought me pain. And I've only ever hurt people as a result of using it. I don't care if Zeke says ghost sex is out of this world. I've sampled that myself, and I will not be going back. This shitty "gift" comes from Dad, and I'm not interested in any of it. I will *not* be a repeat of my father.

"There's nothing here," I say aloud, just for good measure. "I'm not your guy."

And with that, I'm out of there. Lydia will always hate me, and these fucking ghosts will probably always haunt me. But I don't need to stick around for it.

LYDIA

Lydia: So… the architect…

Autumn: ????

Lydia: We were in the library today…

Autumn: ??????

Lydia: After hours…

Autumn: Meet me at Brewed Awakening STAT!

Autumn is already at the corner of Brewed Awakening when I get there. She jumps up from the bench she's sitting on and walks toward me. Around us, the evening is quiet. The only sounds in the chilly autumn air are the laughter drifting in from the bar and the occasional bark of a far-off dog. My mind's still spinning from what just happened, and every single nerve ending in my body is on high alert. I'm a little surprised I could even coax my legs to move after the delicious way Will fucked me with his fingers up against the library wall.

The library wall. *My* library. *Fuck.* I don't know what to make of this.

Which is exactly why Autumn's here.

Ever the fashionista, Autumn's got on a hip-length navy peacoat that nips in at the waist, emphasizing her hourglass figure. I'm normally a bit envious of her voluptuous figure—especially in the boob department—as my hips always seem to look too wide, my chest too small. But then I think about the way Will kneaded my ass barely even an hour ago, cradling my hips in his giant hands like he couldn't get enough, and I feel the tiniest bit... smug?

"Well, *you're* sure glowing," Autumn says with a smirk as I fall into step with her on our normal route around town.

"Oh, stop," I say. "It's dark. I'm not *glowing*."

Autumn scoffs, gesturing to the street lamps around us. "There's plenty of light. I can see just fine. But hey, if you don't want to admit that you let the gorgeous asshole architect—"

"*Autumn*," I hiss, elbowing her hard in the ribs. I lower my voice. "Don't say it so loud."

Autumn's squeal pierces my eardrum. "So you *did*?! You let him fu—"

"No," I jump in, gesturing frantically at her to be quiet. In case she's forgotten, we both live in this town, and I don't want to have to dodge questions. I'm not *ashamed*—I don't think any woman who laid eyes on Will would be—but it's also not a good look to be rolling in the hay with the enemy. "We didn't... sleep together."

Autumn shoots me a side eye. "He may always look like someone just took his parking spot, but he's hot. From the looks of him—and how long it's been since you've had anyone decent—I'd say you *wouldn't* get much sleeping done."

"Wow. Okay. A lot to unpack there. *First* of all, Dylan is decent." Here, Autumn makes a face and starts to protest, but I cut her off. "And *second*, Will and I didn't have sex."

"Oh, yeah? Then what's that guilty look on your face?"

"I mean, we didn't have sex *proper*..."

We stop at the corner, both relishing the coolness of the crisp fall breeze as it swirls around us. Autumn pulls me down onto a bench next to her and turns to me, her green eyes snapping.

"Okay, Lydia. I haven't been fucked in a year, so you owe it to me as my best friend to spill *every single detail*. Got it?"

I blow out my breath. I hate that Autumn is still having to go through her shitty divorce. She shouldn't have to listen to my wins while she's in the middle of such a huge loss of her own. But the way she's leaning back now, arm slung over the back of the bench and wearing this mischievous, eager grin, tells me she's happy for me. And anyway, it's not like I'm getting her happily ever after. It's just sex.

So I launch into it. I tell her how Will came tromping into the mystery section with the ladder balanced on his muscled shoulder, how he started the avalanche of books, and then bolted out of nowhere to keep the ladder from crashing down on my head. I tell her how good his arms looked, holding that ladder up. How he got me up against the wall and made me lose my mind.

I know she asked for all the details, but I hold a few things back. There's something in me that wants them for myself. But I'm not stupid—I know it was a one-time thing. That it *has* to be a one-time thing. Before Dylan, I was never in the habit of letting men get close to me—even ones who aren't involved in demolishing the last connection I have with Mom—and look how *that* turned out. I'm not making that mistake again.

The men in my life don't *disappear*, but they may as well. I barely ever saw Dad, between his nights at the bar and his weekends at work. And that's how it's always been. I'd hoped at the beginning Dylan might be different, but honestly? They're all the same. They can't be bothered—not with me. Will Holloway included.

"Gawwwd," Autumn groans. She lets her head fall back and laughs. "That is so hot. If only that had worked with Patrick. We're *always* pissed at each other."

"I'm sorry," I say, rubbing her arm.

"Don't be—at least I can live vicariously through you. I saw the way Will looked at you at the Farmers Market. Clearly, there were sparks."

My phone buzzes. As I glance down, Autumn, ever the nosy friend, cranes her neck to see who it is and snorts. It's Dylan. I haven't told her he's been calling me all weekend, no doubt to try to explain things away. I haven't answered—yet.

"You've got to be kidding me, Lydia."

I shield the phone screen with a cupped hand, scan the text. Autumn watches me, her green eyes narrowed.

DYLAN: *Hey. You don't want to talk to me. I get it. But I need you to know, Steph's just a friend. There's nothing going on with us. Give me another chance, Lyds. I promise I'll make things right.*

I shove my phone into my pocket. There's no way I'm letting Autumn know what was in that text. She'd probably throw my phone into the nearest trash can—and honestly, I wouldn't blame her. Still, there's a part of me that believes him. It's not like he and the blonde were holding hands or kissing or anything like that...

Maybe he means what he's been saying. Maybe I'm the one who's being harsh.

"Forget about him," Autumn says. "He's history. You just got it on with a sexy architect who's clearly into you."

I let out a harsh laugh, but I'm glad for the change of subject. "Will is *not* into me. He was just thinking with the wrong head. It was like once we started arguing, all the tension that's been building between us finally erupted."

"You mean *he* erupted," Autumn says, giving me a smirk.

"Um..."

Autumn sits up straight. "Do you mean to tell me that sexy motherfucker finger banged you until you *came*, and then didn't so much as ask for anything in return?"

I wince at her description. "Pretty much."

"And you think he's not into you." Autumn throws her head back and cackles.

"I don't *think*—I *know*. The only thing Will Holloway wants is to butter me up, so I'll stop nagging him about changing the design plans."

"Well," Autumn says, standing from the bench. She links her arm with mine. "Regardless. You know what they say:

Keep your friends close and your enemies closer. I'd say a good old blow job would fall under the 'closer' category, right?"

I elbow her playfully in the ribs. "Gross."

The problem is, sucking Will Holloway's cock *doesn't* sound gross. At all. Especially after today, with the way he knew exactly how to stroke me, inside and out.

But it doesn't matter. Will's already ripping out a piece of me with his stupid project. No way am I going to let him break my heart, too.

thirteen

Zeke: Will. What's for dinner?

Benji: Zeke, this is the group chat.

Zeke: I know. Will won't answer his phone.
Benji, tell Will to answer his phone.

Benji: Will, answer your phone.

Will: Holy shot, you guys. Be home in 10.

Will: *Shot

Will: *Shot

Will: OMG SHIT

"**B**ro. You smell like sex."

It's the first thing Zeke says to me when I walk in the door. I dump my briefcase near the entryway and stalk into the kitchen. He's leaning backward on his elbows against the counter, his phone lying face up next to him.

"Damn, Will!" A rich, gravelly voice comes from the speaker of Zeke's phone, and I instantly recognize it as our brother, Benji. "What's the story? You get some?"

"Hi, Benji," I say, ignoring their ribbing.

"It's that librarian," Zeke announces. "I'd bet money on it."

"Money you don't have," Benji says. He beat me to it.

"Well, I'd have it after I win this bet," Zeke insists. He hoists himself up, so he's sitting on the counter. "Because I'm right. You can't see his face right now, Benj, but Will looks guilty as fuck."

Benji laughs. "Okay, but I think I missed something. What's this about a librarian?"

"Nothing," I say. "Zeke's just being an asshole."

"I mean, guilty as charged about the asshole thing," Zeke says. "But you know how Will's in charge of renovating the Hawthorne Bay library? Apparently, he and the assistant librarian—who's really nice, by the way, offered to help me with my resume—hate each other. But Will's got the hots for her."

"I do *not*," I grumble as I pull out pans to make something for dinner.

Zeke sniffs the air. "That's not what the scent you're giving off says."

At this, Benji bursts out laughing. "You can't hide it, Will. Not with Zeke there on scout duty."

"Fine. You guys are such dipshits," I say. There's no use

bothering to hide it anymore. My brothers will stop at nothing.

"So you like her?" Benji asks.

God. Leave it to Benji to get straight to the feelings stuff.

"No, actually," I say.

Zeke arches an eyebrow. "Then how come you went out of your way to say hi to her at the Farmers Market? And bought her those caramel apples?"

"Because I feel bad, okay? She's got... I don't know, some weird connection to the library and wants to keep it the way it is. Something about her childhood. Her mom."

Zeke looks at me. "Her mom? What, like a ghost thing?"

I shake my head. "I don't think so. She's never let on that she... has the sight."

Curse is the word I'd normally use for this *gift* we've all got, but Benji gets weird when I call it that, so I swallow it back.

"Did you also bang her because you felt bad for her?" Benji asks.

"No. We got into an argument and—"

"Yeeessssss," Zeke cuts in with a slow clap. "I'm on board with a good hate fuck!"

I just shake my head at him and grunt. I didn't actually *fuck* Lydia, at least not in the way he's thinking. The way every single fiber of my body was begging me to. And I'm still not exactly sure why I didn't. All I know is, in that moment, with her back against the wall and my hand up her skirt, I didn't want to take more from her than I already am. It'd be a dick move.

"It was a one-time thing. And anyway, we didn't fuck."

"Okay, he likes her," Benji announces, his voice tinny as it erupts from the phone speaker.

Zeke raises his eyebrows. He looks pointedly at me from his perch on the counter even as he speaks to Benji. "Well, he's fucking up that library she's weirdly attached to, so I'd say he'll have plenty of opportunities for hate fucking."

I don't answer, just start cracking eggs into a pan. God knows Zeke's not going to do it.

"Yeah, what are you going to do about that?" Benji asks me.

"Do about what?"

"The fact that you clearly like this chick, but you're still in charge of the project that's, by the sounds of it, going to sever a connection she has with her mother. Which, by the way—what's the story *there*?"

This is way more than I bargained for when I walked in the door. And, truth be told, it's way more than came to my mind as I let myself give into my primal side this afternoon. Because there's no getting around it. I was thinking with my dick. But leave it to Benji to cut right through the noise.

"Fuck, man," I say. I slide a spatula under one of the eggs to check the bottoms. "I don't know. I don't know about any of it, okay? I wasn't thinking. It was a stupid thing to do."

"No offense, Will, but it sounds kind of irresponsible," Benji says. I can hear the skepticism in his voice, despite the fuzziness of the speaker.

Zeke slaps the counter. "Benjamin! Shots fired."

I'm already tensing at that word. *Irresponsible*. As if being irresponsible is a luxury I've ever had. I'm half tempted to tell him that if it's irresponsibility he wants to talk about, he's got the wrong brother. He knows very well I've had to be the backbone of this family.

"Well, I'm just saying…" Benji continues. "That's your career you're fucking with. Didn't you say Ethan Wilde's on that board? If you're still trying to win him over for that housing project, banging the librarian doesn't exactly scream professionalism. And don't even get me started on how you're fucking with this woman's *feelings*…"

I close my eyes. This is not what I need. My body hasn't forgotten that I didn't get a release this afternoon, and I'm this close to lashing out at my brothers, no matter how well intentioned they—well, at least Benji—might be.

"I don't need a lecture, Benj."

"Alright. You do you. But hey. Maybe there's something you can do to soften the blow of the library renovation? You're good at restoring shit. You wouldn't have got this gig if you weren't."

I slide a plate of eggs toward Zeke and toss him a fork, which lands on the counter with a clatter. I cut into my eggs, frowning. "What do you mean?"

"You know," Benji says. "Like, compromise a little. Pick a piece of the library to preserve—a sort of homage to the building's history—and add it to the plans. She'd probably like it, and it'd be cool regardless."

I pull myself up onto the counter next to Zeke. The wheels in my mind are already turning. I'm thinking back to the stakeholder meeting, where Lydia all but begged me to change the project plans. She'd talked about her childhood then, hadn't she? Something about sliding down the banister in the foyer, pretending she was a princess on a quest?

That's it. The banister. She pointed it out to me on our walkthrough as well.

Right now, the plans we drew up have the banister replaced with something sleek and modern. But it's the floor plan and the structure, the shelving and lighting—the computer lab—that the board really wants to modernize. As long as I can make sure the main floor is wheelchair accessible, I might be able to keep the banister there...

Benji's got a point. Preserving a historic piece of the library, especially one that plays such a fond part in Lydia's childhood memories, is something I can do for her. It might even earn me a little artistic credit with the board. Showing off my range to Ethan Wilde can't hurt.

"Interesting," I say, scratching the scruff on my chin. "That's not a bad idea."

Zeke shoots me a malicious grin. "She might even let you fuck her for real."

"*That* is not the problem," I huff. "Some of us have self restraint."

But even after Zeke ends the call with Benji and heads out the door to god knows where, his words still echo through my head. I keep thinking back to that mask Lydia so expertly slid over her face once the rapture was over and she realized what the fuck we were doing. How she all but pushed me out the door.

Maybe Zeke's right. Maybe the reason it ended where it did this afternoon wasn't because of *me*, but because of her. Would I have kept going if she'd wanted to? If she hadn't turned suddenly icy, pulling her skirt back down and shoving me away?

I honestly don't know. I thought it was obvious that Lydia hated me—and that I found her annoying as shit—but do people who hate each other really do what we just did this afternoon? Zeke seems to think so, but this kind of thing is entirely out of my wheelhouse.

One thing's for sure: I know I'm no good for her. I'm no good for *any* woman. But as I stand here in the empty kitchen, loading the dishwasher, there's a weird sort of sinking in my gut when I realize that Lydia really may *not* want anything to do with me.

And I don't know how the fuck to feel about that.

LYDIA

Autumn: Any developments??

Lydia: I don't know what you're talking about.

Autumn: Oh, come on. I thought you were going to keep your enemy close!

Lydia: No, YOU said that. I'm keeping my enemy far, far away.

Autumn: Girl…

Will and I don't talk for five days after what happened in the mystery section.

Two of the days were the weekend when —thank *god*—I didn't run into him around town, but for three days since then, he's only been in and out of the library, and we've been completely cool to each other. We barely even say hi in greeting and only flash brief, civil smiles when absolutely necessary. We're like awkward high schoolers, pretending to be busy when one of us walks in the room. If Nancy's noticed anything, she hasn't said so. But then again, she probably just chalks it up to the renovation. It's not exactly a secret that I don't like what Will was hired to do.

But I haven't been able to get his touch out of my head. The way his huge hands felt around my waist, how his kiss was somehow gruff and tender at the same time. And the other stuff... I'd be lying if I said my mind hadn't strayed there while I was in the shower. That I hadn't touched myself while thinking of the way his fingers had grazed my clit.

And I hate that I'm thinking about it now while I sit behind the library desk, scanning a shit ton of books before I return them to the shelves. I didn't say a word to Will today when he strode through here with some engineer or other. Hell, I barely even looked up when I saw him come in this morning.

But I did notice how good he looked when I stole a glance after he'd turned away. His broad back, shoulders straining against his t-shirt as he points out all the wiring and electrical stuff to the guy he's brought in. The scruff on his chin that felt so surprisingly good when he kissed me. Just looking at him makes me ache between my legs.

I jump as Nancy's voice breaks into my thoughts.

"You feeling any better about the renovation? This Will Holloway's a damned good architect, you know. He'll do the town proud."

I look up, glance around the faded, yet homey space around me. It's hard to wrap my head around the fact it'll be changing so much in only a few short months. While I have to admit the plans Will has drawn up for the place are pretty impressive, they're a clear deviation from the building's original features.

The wooden framed skylights, the elevator and automatic door at the front entrance, and the all new glass-walled computer lab are, admittedly, nice in theory—just not for *Mom's* library. This stuff is an automatic no-go for the Hawthorne Bay Historical Society. And they're not even keeping my fucking banister.

"Well," I say. "I still don't know why the board wants to move so far from the historical authenticity of the building. It's a shame, if you ask me."

"Oh, cheer up," Nancy says, giving the desk next to me a playful rap. "You'll get used to it. You'll see. And anyway, your mother would've loved it. She'd have wanted it to better suit the needs of the community."

It's on the tip of my tongue to tell her she has no clue what my mother would have wanted, but I manage to stop myself. The only thing worse than the library not being the library anymore is the library not being the library *and* I'm out of my job there. I've got to tread carefully.

I fake a smile. "Maybe you're right."

"I'm at least glad to know you're keeping an open mind," Nancy continues, beaming. "Because I keep meaning to mention—Ethan thought it'd be a good idea to have Will help us man the fundraising booth at the fall festival. You know, so in case anyone in town has questions about the renovation, they'll be able to ask the architect himself. I have to say I agree with him—I think it'll get everyone excited."

A cold wave of panic rips through me. I'm more than happy to help Nancy man the library's fundraising booth—in fact, I've been brainstorming ideas on how to spin our book sale—but *god*. They're seriously going to make me spend *more* time with this scruffy, arrogant man outside of work hours? Will's already taking up way more of my mental real estate than he's entitled to—and working next to him with only Nancy as protection is not going to help matters.

I'm about to protest when someone clears their throat from across the room.

Well, speak of the devil.

Of *course* it's Will. He's leaning against the doorframe, hands shoved deep in his pockets, looking as infuriatingly sexy as ever.

I stifle a groan. I hate that he has a key, that he can let himself in whenever the hell he wants. But when Nancy sees Will, her face lights up. It's clear this guy has my boss wrapped completely around his little finger.

Goddamnit. I can't be thinking about Will's fingers. Not right now—not ever. Our little... incident... was a mistake I will *not* be allowing myself to make again.

My tone is cool as I stare him down. "Yes?"

"Am I interrupting?"

"I mean, it *is* the middle of the work day," I say, breaking his gaze to flip my eyes back to the books I'm scanning.

"Nonsense," Nancy chides, giving a nervous laugh. She

casts me a warning look. "I was just telling Lydia that it'll be the three of us working the library booth at the fall festival, which she was very excited to hear. We'll have a ball, I'm sure!"

Even across the room, I see Will's blue eyes twinkle, and *ugh*—this asshole just *winked* at me. I don't even bother to refute Nancy's version of events because what good would that do? The lazy grin Will's wearing as he walks toward us tells me he already knows I am *not* excited about the news Nancy just dropped on me.

"Definitely," Will agrees. He runs a huge hand through his tousled hair, and I have to look down. I'm suddenly remembering how his honey-blond locks fell into his eyes as he thrust his fingers into me just a room away from here.

"Anyway," Nancy says, her glow returning. "What can we help you with?"

I can feel Will's eyes still on me as he steps forward, but I keep my own fixed on the barcode of the Stephen King book I'm scanning. *Beep.*

"Well, I've got something to show Lydia, actually, but if she's too busy I can find a different time…"

"Oh, don't be silly!" Nancy swipes my stack of books toward her and gives me a little shove. "I'll take over here, Lydia."

With no excuse left, I rise from my chair and stalk out from behind the desk. I avoid Will's gaze even as I approach him, making sure not to come too close. The last thing I want to do is let myself start thinking about that solid fucking chest of his.

"What do you need?" I ask, keeping my tone as even as possible.

Will gives a low chuckle, like it's exactly the reaction he expected from me. He tips his head toward the doorway, and I follow him out to the foyer, arms crossed tightly over my chest.

"Thought it might be easier to envision out here," he says, slipping his phone from his pocket.

"Envision what? The gutting you're planning for this poor old building?"

"Jesus, woman. Can you give it a rest?"

"*Wow*, you're a charmer."

Will gives me a hard look but ignores me, his eyes softening again as he swipes through his phone. He shakes his head, thrusts the phone toward me. "Here. It's probably hard to see on this tiny screen but I tried to do it justice. It wasn't in the original plans, but I managed to get it cleared with everyone on the board..."

I frown, but I'm curious now, so I take the phone. It takes me a minute to figure out what I'm seeing, but when I do, I stop short, my breath catching in my throat.

Because there, on the screen of Will's phone, is my banister.

Peering at the screen, I zoom in to see the rendering in detail, my eyes flicking between the current real-life foyer and the one that Will's envisioned. The automatic door is still there, as is the elevator shaft and the paneling along the walls. But I'm shocked to see the way he's managed to tie them in with the design, making the majestic staircase and the original banister—the one I loved so much as a child—the center of the foyer.

In Will's rendering, the banister is polished and shiny, stained a deep, rustic cherry color that makes it come alive. The decorative carvings that spiral up and down the railings are sharp and clear—a far cry to the state of the banister now, with all its chips and divots. He's taken a beat-up piece of history and breathed new life into it.

I look up at Will, a little awestruck. I gesture to the phone. "You're... going to do this?"

Will nods. For a split second, I think I see something in his gaze. Something almost searching. But then he speaks, and I lose sight of it. "Yeah. You like it? Does it pass the Lydia test?"

"It's beautiful," I say. Because it is.

"Is it... how you remember it? From when you were a kid?"

There's that searching again, only in his voice this time. I nod, bringing my eyes to his. It's the most words we've spoken to each other since last Thursday.

"Definitely. Only better, honestly. It looks... gorgeous."

He flashes me a grin that makes my knees weak. "Good."

We're quiet a moment, both staring at the phone screen. I'm not sure what else to say. As thankful as I am, as impressed as I am with the rendering, it's only a small piece of the building. Preservation of a banister does not a historical landmark make. But it's something—and right now, something is all I need. It means there's hope.

Will's voice breaks into the silence. "Hey, can I ask you something?"

I look up at him to see him watching me closely. "Sure."

"I don't know exactly how to word this, but... what's your deal with this place? Why are you so desperate to keep it the way it is?"

I sigh. Then I take a deep breath and tell him something I've never told anyone except Autumn. Because no one's ever bothered to ask.

"My mom died of cancer when I was ten. My dad... he couldn't take it. He sort of checked out, left me to fend for myself. He was *there*, I guess, like physically *there*, but mentally... emotionally..." I trail off because it sucks thinking about it. "I used to come here every day. While my dad was drunk in front of the TV, or at the bar or whatever, I came here to feel safe. And to feel close to my mom. She used to be the librarian here, and she and the building and all my memories of being loved are kind of... wrapped up together."

Will looks through the big front window, out at the street. Mounds of crisp, orange leaves litter the sidewalks, and he stands, studying them. He doesn't say anything, so I continue.

"I kind of always hoped... I don't know, that I'd *feel* her somehow. That she'd send me some kind of message. I know that probably sounds stupid."

He looks at me sharply. "It doesn't sound stupid."

"No?"

"No."

I sigh. "Well, it doesn't matter. I've hung around here all these years—hell, even became the assistant librarian—and nothing. I'm probably just crazy."

Will gives a weird sort of chuckle. "I doubt that."

In this moment, with him standing there in the middle of the mid-afternoon sunlight streaming through the windows, I have the sudden thought that the only thing I feel truly crazy about is him. I push the thought down.

It's only a thought, after all. It doesn't mean it's real.

"I'm still holding out hope I'll see her—feel her?—one last time. But once this place is renovated…" I trail off, shrugging. "It won't be the same place. I don't think she'll be here."

Will is looking at me strangely, with an expression I can't read. He's probably listening to me talk, essentially drone on about ghosts or spirits or whatever you want to call it, and thinking to himself what an idiot I am.

Even *I* think I sound idiotic, saying this stuff out loud. I need to learn when to shut it. It's clear I haven't been able to grieve my mom properly.

Will clears his throat, interrupting my thoughts. "Well, I don't know about any of that, but I'm happy to keep you in the loop regarding the plans and design. As you know, we've got a lot of the stuff already nailed down, but if there are any small, yet meaningful alterations I can make—like this one, keeping in that banister—feel free to let me know."

I raise my eyebrows. "Does Ethan Wilde know about this offer?"

Will gives a harsh laugh. "Don't push your luck, Chandler. Give me your phone."

I don't even know what to think anymore, so I hand over my phone and watch as Will saves his number to my contacts. When he passes my phone back to me, I feel the brush of his rough fingers against mine and my stomach flutters.

"I'll see you around," Will says.

As he gives me a nod and heads out the door, I turn and walk numbly back to my desk. I don't know what *any* of that just was, but my stomach's light and jumpy, and I realize suddenly that I'm not mad about it. I'm not mad about it at all.

fifteen

LYDIA

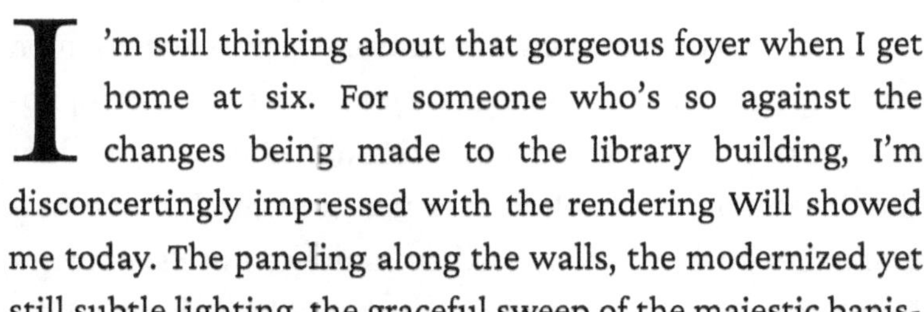

I'm still thinking about that gorgeous foyer when I get home at six. For someone who's so against the changes being made to the library building, I'm disconcertingly impressed with the rendering Will showed me today. The paneling along the walls, the modernized yet still subtle lighting, the graceful sweep of the majestic banister, commanding all the attention away from the elevator shaft and automatic door. It isn't lost on me that he reworked the design for *me*. He listened.

But still—that damn elevator. That freaking door. That *computer* lab. There's a rock in my stomach when I think about it, because I *know* it's what's best for the community. Only a privileged bitch would turn up her nose at making the library a more accessible place to the public. But that's exactly what I'm doing. And I kind of hate myself for it.

I just... can't let go. I can't let go of this place. Or of Mom, and our memories together there, and her dream of having it recognized as the historical landmark it's always been. She loved this place even more than I did. I guess it's a good sign that I'm starting to chip away at Will Holloway, get him to see my side a bit more. He's at least listening, which is more than anyone on the board has done so far.

I just need to keep at him, keep making my case. I'm nothing if not determined.

I throw my bag on the counter and pull out the Nespresso machine. I know it's evening, but I'm too up in my head to even think about going to bed anytime soon. A little coffee will give me a jolt of energy to help me dissect the never-ending stream of thoughts. Or at least, I hope so.

As the water heats up, I lean back against the counter, scrolling through my phone. Instagram is the same cacophonous mire it always is, but I flick through it anyway, glad for the distraction as the Nespresso machine gurgles. Bookstagrammers gushing about cowboy romance novels, amateur fashionistas with better style sense than I'll ever have, stupid memes from the library science account I followed in grad school. Some of those still make me laugh.

But then there's a story that makes me suck in my breath. Actually, I flick right past it, and only when it registers *what that just was* do I scroll back to see it for real.

And I was right. My split second first glance hunch was right.

There's a couple on the shore, waves crashing behind them, who are all over each other in a way that, were they not fully clothed, would probably get their accounts banned. And yeah—the account who posted it? It's fucking Dylan.

He's holding the girl like she jumped on him, hands squeezing her jean-clad ass, and her legs are wrapped around him. And unfortunately for us unsuspecting scrollers, they're turned to the side—so we can see every bit of their full-on make-out sesh. The girl's long blond hair tumbles down her shoulders, and although I can't see her face very well—and nor do I want to try—I'd bet anything it's the blonde from the Farmers Market. The one he introduced as his "friend".

I tear my eyes away from the photo to read the caption, and my heart sinks further into my stomach.

Truly the love of my life. Happiest man in the world.

God, *fuck* him. It's been—what? Four months since we broke up? I'm not trying to judge how fast people fall in love, but for someone who was just two weeks ago trying to booty call me, asking me to give him a second chance, his phrasing is more than a little suspect. And it makes my fucking blood boil.

Who the *fuck* does he think he is? And what does he take *me* for? Some kind of side piece he can mess around with on a whim, keep in the wings for when he's not feeling the love of his life so much? Fuck that shit. I am *so* glad I never answered that goddamn text of his.

That was the text that Will—

Something in my stomach gives a little flip. I barely know the guy, but I'd be willing to bet Will Holloway would never pull a stunt like this. Granted, he'd be too standoffish to really care about someone in the first place, but from what I've seen of him, I doubt there'd be much messing around.

And... thanks to him, I happen to have his number.

Well, shit.

I barely even let myself think about what I'm doing as I flick out of Instagram and head to my contacts. This is ridiculous—*I* am ridiculous—but I've got to do *something*. I know I can't just sit here all night, crying alone into my espresso. I need company. I need a distraction. And I tell myself it's for precisely that reason when I fire off a text to Will.

Hey. It's Lydia Chandler. You around?

I see the little blue dots dancing almost immediately. I'm a little embarrassed by the way it makes my heart jump.

Sure. What's up?

I pause. I don't know how I want to play this. I don't even know what my goal here is, just that I need out of this house and that I need a distraction. I decide I may as well be honest.

I need to get out, get some fresh air. You wanna join?

This time, I see the read receipt pop up, but the blue dots don't appear. My stomach clenches, and I close my eyes. He's clearly seen my message but is taking his time to respond—if he even *does* respond to something so out of left field. *Way to appear over eager, Lydia. So attractive.*

But then my phone buzzes, and my eyes pop open.

Actually, I'm headed to the shore. It's really nice this time of night. Meet me at the library and we can walk over together?

I only pretend to think before replying.

Sure. See you in ten.

My heart's still pounding from the photo I just saw five minutes ago, but now my stomach's fluttering, too. I try to push them both down, get my head screwed on straight.

Dylan's not my boyfriend—he's my ex. He can do what he wants. And this thing with Will isn't a date. It's a distraction. A little fresh air and conversation will reel me back into my senses. At least, this is what I tell myself as I grab my coat and hat and head out the door.

But I'm beginning to think I'm lying to myself just as much as Dylan has been.

sixteen

LYDIA

Will's already waiting on a bench outside the library when I walk up. He's changed his clothes since this afternoon, and it's the first time I've seen him in something other than a sweaty t-shirt. He's rolled the sleeves of his flannel shirt up to the forearms, exposing his tanned skin underneath, and I seriously almost swoon. I can't let myself look at his hands without my mind straying to other places.

He stands as I approach. "Ready?"

"Sure."

We head off toward the shore in silence, neither of us knowing what to say to the other. He doesn't mention the randomness of my text, and I don't offer an explanation. There's clearly something between us, whether or not we've acknowledged it, but I have yet to figure out what it is.

"So you come down to the shore a lot?" I ask. I know my attempt at conversation is lame, but I don't care. It's better than silence.

"Sometimes, yeah. It's nice to just sit there and listen to the waves crashing. Makes all the other stuff feel small."

I glance over at him. "What other stuff?"

"You know." He shrugs. "Family. Money. Regrets. Existential angst."

"Regrets, huh? You got a lot of those?" I'm half playing, half really wanting to know.

Will raises an eyebrow. "I've got a few, sure. Who doesn't?"

"Fair enough."

The leaves crunch beneath our feet as we walk. I smell the ocean before I see it, the salty air stinging my nose. And then water comes into view, vast and wide and shimmering beneath the setting sun.

I follow Will as he makes his way down the path, then steps off into the sand and continues up the shoreline. When he finds the perfect spot, he stops and looks out at the sun that's now melting into the span of dark, silvery water.

"The other thing I like to do," he says, "is make a bonfire. Just a small one, of course—but it gets chilly out here."

We gather branches from the trees that line the shore. Once we've each got an armful, we toss them in a heap on the sand, and Will pulls a few pages of crumpled newspaper out of his satchel, which he balls up and throws on the pile. Then, fishing a lighter out of his jeans pocket, Will waves me out of the way of the wind and sets the pile of sticks ablaze.

The fire starts slowly, crackling in the quiet of the evening air. Will waits to see if it'll catch. And it does—it's only a moment before the tiny flames start licking their way up the branches, dancing and flickering in tandem as the crisp autumn breeze sweeps across the shore.

Will drops to the blanket he shook out on the sand for us. He looks at the sea, sighing heavily. "Now, *this*. This is what I needed."

I murmur my agreement. As the sun melts into the ocean, dissipating into a pool of shimmering, rippling color, I find myself loosening. It's as though the pent up, stuffed down tension in my body has been swept out with the tide and I'm simply free floating. At this moment, I'm not even wishing for Dylan's downfall anymore.

"It's so calming," I say. "Thanks for inviting me to come along."

He looks over at me. He's leaning back on his elbows, his long legs stretched out in front of him in the sand. "No problem."

We're quiet a moment, and then he says, "My mom loved the shore."

I wonder about his use of the past tense, but I leave it alone. "Oh, yeah?"

"Yeah. She used to take my siblings and me down here in the summers. We grew up in Boston, but she was from here —from Hawthorne Bay."

I'm surprised. Hawthorne Bay is a pretty small place. I always assumed that since I'd never heard of any Holloways, Will had no prior connection to my town—that he was just another opportunist come to take advantage of the Salem tourism boom.

As if reading my thoughts, Will continues. "After she died six years ago, I was kind of lost. Somehow wound up here.

Bought a house, moved my business. Sort of started over, I guess."

"Why here?"

He stares out at the water for a minute, as if weighing his response. "Remember how you said you stick around the library because you're hoping to, like, feel your mom?"

I nod.

"It's like that."

"And?"

"And what?"

"Have you felt her?"

Will turns to look at me. I see him swallow, the muscles in his throat working. "No."

He holds my gaze for a minute, and then breaks eye contact, looking down at the fire. He grabs a stick and pokes it into the embers. The fire crackles, flames biting anew at the branches. Then he settles himself back on the sand, stretches his entire, muscled body out so he's lying completely flat beneath the purple sky. I see his chest heaving as he breathes in and out.

"Come down here," he says.

I hesitate. I'm already unsure about whatever this is between us, and lying down next to him in the sand feels a little like—*ahem*—sleeping with the enemy.

But he looks so peaceful stretched out below me. Just... utterly calm. And I want that, too. Looking at the way his broad chest rises and falls is already making me feel things, but I can keep a handle on myself—right? I'm a grown ass woman.

I lie down beside him. The sand is soft beneath me as I

stare up at the darkening sky, fully aware of how warm Will's solid form is next to me. I have the sudden urge to roll over into him, tuck myself into his warmth, find his hand in the darkness—but obviously I push it down. I've been here before. I know how this goes. And it doesn't end with a man sticking around. My dad didn't stick around, and Dylan didn't stick around. Hell, *people* don't stick around.

"Told you this'd be nice," Will says.

I steal a glance at him. His eyes are closed, and there's a small half smile on his lips.

"You were right. I can see why you come out here."

"Mmm."

We're quiet again. The only sound is the crackling of the bonfire, the rhythmic lapping of the waves on the shoreline.

I push myself up to my elbows and look down at Will. His eyes are still closed.

"Thank you, by the way. For redrawing the plans around the banister. I'm not sure I told you properly this afternoon."

His eyes blink open. I think he's about to say something, but before I'm even fully aware of what I'm doing, I'm brushing my lips to his stubbled cheek, and a split second later his mouth is on mine and his huge hands are around my waist, pulling me on top of him.

Will runs his hands up my ribcage, slides them up my breasts and to my shoulders, and then plants them on either side of my face. His touch is firm, assertive, as he pulls my mouth toward him. He kisses me ravenously, every bit as hungry as he was that day in the mystery section. His hands tangle through my wind-swept hair.

"Fuck," he groans into my mouth.

I pull back, still straddling him. We're both fully clothed, but having his muscled body between my legs is doing things to me. If I were to slide myself down even just a bit...

I don't have to finish the thought because Will does it for me. He picks me up and sets my ass down right on his package, which I can tell even through his jeans is rock hard. I lock eyes with him, rocking my hips back and forth over the solid mass of his erection. He closes his eyes, his hands still on my waist, rocking himself in rhythm with me.

He moves his hands beneath my shirt, his fingers skimming my stomach as they slide upward again. He keeps his gaze on me the entire time, like he's making sure it's what I want, and he draws in a sharp breath when his hands finally reach their destination inside my bra. My nipples are hard beneath his palms.

My voice is low, almost a whisper. "Will."

"Yeah?"

He closes his eyes. He's rolling my nipple between his index finger and thumb, and the sensation is making it hard for me to think. But I want to get this out. Because I can already sense that whatever line we're about to cross here is one we won't be able to inch back over.

"This isn't very professional."

It's not how I intended it to come out, and know I sound like some kind of prudish schoolmarm, but Will chuckles low and soft and I feel his chest rumble beneath me. He pushes himself up to the heels of his hands and makes eye contact, the flickering flames of the bonfire next to us reflecting in his pupils.

"Sure isn't, beautiful. So if you want this, you better stop talking before I start thinking."

And with that, his mouth crashes into mine and he's kissing me so hard I can barely breathe. As his tongue sweeps through my mouth, he wraps his arms around me and pulls the hem of my sweater up and over my head. I shrug free of it, my skin bristling at the chill of the night air.

Will's hands are rough as one braces behind my head, the other sliding my bra strap down and moving to my breast. He cups it in his hand, breaking our kiss to lean down and take my nipple in his mouth. He sucks it hard, and I shudder at the wetness of his mouth, marveling at the ferocity of his movements. Because Will isn't being gentle or tender. He's fucking hungry, and I want him to make a meal of me.

So when he moves his mouth to my neck and rasps in my ear for me to lie back, I comply. I slip down off his lap, and lean back onto the blanket, unhooking my bra and tossing it aside. The breeze drifting in from the sea is chilly on my now bare skin. Will's kneeling in the sand, looking down at me spread out before him. His eyes rake over my chest and he sucks in his breath.

"Fuck, Lydia," he says. "You're so fucking beautiful. Lying there like some kind of painting."

He strips off his shirt, and I'm honestly floored as I watch his biceps ripple with the movement. He's kneeling there in front of me, the firelight flickering on his fucking chiseled chest, and he thinks *I'm* some kind of painting? Has this guy looked in a mirror?

"I could say the same," I murmur.

He scoffs, brushing the compliment away like it doesn't matter and tosses me his shirt.

"You're cold—drape that over you. But just for now. After this, I'm going to want to feel every inch of that creamy skin of yours against me."

His hands move to unbutton my jeans. He slides them down around my hips, then my thighs, my knees and ankles, my feet. With my panties still on, he kneels between my legs and spreads my thighs apart. He's so fucking gorgeous, kneeling there between my legs, that it's all I can do not to lunge at his zipper and set him loose, rub my already throbbing core against what's under the outline I can still see against his pant leg. Instead, I watch as he leans down to press his lips to the dampness on my panties.

"So fucking wet," Will murmurs. "So fucking delicious. And I haven't even tasted you yet."

He moves his mouth to the waistband of my panties and swipes his tongue beneath it, sliding it along my hip bone and making me shudder. Then, catching the lace of my panties in his teeth, he drags them downward, over my hips and thighs, until I can feel the chill of the night on my most sensitive skin. He spreads my thighs again, baring me to him completely.

I close my eyes. This can't be happening. This man I'm supposed to hate—who just a couple weeks ago walked into my life to destroy something so dear to me—is now kneeling shirtless above my spread legs, gazing down at my naked sex like he just won the lottery.

There's a part of me that's flinching in embarrassment,

wanting to clamp my legs closed so this beautiful man can't get any nearer to me than he already has. His fingers inside me in the library was one thing. That time was rushed and frantic. A mistake. This, though? Next to the crashing waves with only the dark around us? It feels terrifyingly intimate. And deliberate.

But when I open my eyes and meet Will's gaze as he moves his mouth to my sex, all reason flies out the window. I want him so badly I can barely stand it. He swipes his tongue clear up the middle of my core, holding my gaze as he does.

"You want it?" I can feel the vibrations of his words as he murmurs them against my cunt.

"Fuck yes," I say.

Will dips his head back down and I feel the warmth and wet of his tongue as he drags it up and down the folds of my pussy. When he reaches my clit, he sucks it gently, teasing my bud with the very tip of his tongue. A moan rises in my throat, and my thighs turn to jelly as he continues, the strokes of his tongue deft and warm. When he thrusts his tongue inside me, my hips buck and he pins them down with his huge, spread hands. His fingertips graze my clit as he tongue fucks me, and all the while a warm, gentle pressure is building in my pelvis. I tangle my fingers in his hair, trying to rock my hips against his face.

Just when I feel that delicious pressure start to creep toward the edge, Will draws back. My fingers grab for his hair, desperate to pull him back in. I'm so fucking close. He can't stop now.

"Will..." My voice comes out like a whine. I push myself up to my elbows.

Will lets out a low laugh as he rises back up to his knees and starts working at his belt buckle. The grin on his face is absolutely taunting. "Oh, you wanted to come like that, huh?"

"Yes, actually," I say, indignant. "Fuck y—"

But my voice cuts off as Will unzips his jeans and leans toward me, pushing me backward again onto the blanket. Still gazing at me, he tugs his jeans and boxers deftly down his hips—and finally, *finally* I'm about to see what I've known all along was there. I break eye contact in time to see his cock spring free, to watch as he brings the smooth skin of it to brush against my inner thighs.

He's as long and thick as I thought he was.

Fuck.

I can smell the salt in his hair as he bends his mouth to my ear. "Did you really think I'd stop at eating your pussy, Lydia?"

"I don't know," I murmur.

And it's true. I don't know what the fuck I thought. I don't know what the fuck *to* think. I only that Will Holloway's rock hard cock is bobbing between my legs, and the only thing I want is for him to fuck me silly.

Will clucks his tongue. "Well, let's think. I've fucked you with my fingers. Now I've fucked you with my tongue. You know what's left?"

My voice shakes, but I force myself to look him in the eye as I answer. "Your cock."

"That's exactly right," Will growls. He reaches down to slap his dick against my thigh. The sharp sting is electric.

"The only thing left is to fuck you with my cock. Do you want that?"

"Yes," I choke out. He won't shut up, and my sex is absolutely pulsing with need.

"I've got a condom in my wallet. I want to watch you touch yourself while I put it on."

I may as well be in a trance, because I obey without a second thought. My hand moves between my legs as Will fishes his wallet from the pocket of his discarded jeans and tears open the foil packet with his teeth. He eyes me hungrily as he rolls the condom down his length.

I meet his eyes, my own fingers still circling my clit. It feels good, but not as good as he does.

"Will, can you just…"

"Put it in?"

"*Yes*. Fuck."

A smile plays on his mouth as he looks down to rub the fat head of his cock against me, teasing my entrance. I can already feel my wetness glazing him as he nudges himself ever so slightly inside, then pulls back out. There's no way I'm the only one he's driving wild right now. This has got to be killing him, too.

"Okay, Lydia. I'll put it in," Will says. He's hovering above me, his cock poised at my opening. He leans down to growl into my ear. "And not only will I put it in—but I'm going to fuck you deep. And hard. And rough. Just like I've been wanting to since I saw that fucking text. Just like you deserve."

And then he slams into me. I gasp with the quick flash of pain that comes with his size, but it's over in a second, and my pussy welcomes him, molding around his length. He thrusts in and out in deep, long strokes, angling himself so that his tip hits inside in exactly the right place. Gripping his ass, I pull him in deeper and he groans.

"Fuck, Lydia." His voice is low and rough in my ear. "You're so fucking tight. So wet for me. You've been waiting for this, haven't you?"

I moan out something that I think sounds like *yes*, and it's only after I do that it fully dawns on me how true it is. Because this *is* what I wanted—isn't it? Will Holloway is a brooding, selfish prick, but just looking at him makes my panties wet. Where that leaves us, I don't know. But right now, with his erection pumping in and out of me, I don't care.

"And you know what else," Will murmurs, his breaths coming in pants now as he keeps the rhythm with his hips. "Makes me wonder... about that other guy. The one who texted you. He's the same guy from the Farmers Market, isn't he? I bet he didn't stretch you out like this. Didn't fill you up with his cock like I do."

The heat is building in my lower abdomen again as my mind flashes on that fucking Instagram photo. Dylan is the last person I want to think about in this moment. In fact, if I'm honest with myself, I texted Will precisely to *not* have to think about Dylan for a couple of hours. Probably because I knew something like this would end up happening.

So I say nothing, just run my hands along the muscled slope of Will's back and close my eyes.

"Hmm." Will gives one last thrust, then slides out of me.

No. Fucking. Way. If he thinks he's going to bring me this far only to—

"Turn over," Will commands. He snaps his fingers, then gives my ass a slap as I roll over onto my stomach and peer back at him. "On all fours. It's time you were fucked by someone who knows how."

seventeen

WILL

*F*uck.

Lydia's on her hands and knees in front of me, and the sweeping curve of her ass is absolutely glorious in the flickering light of the fire. She's looking back at me, and her eyes hold mine, almost like she's afraid that if she doesn't, I'll suddenly throw on my clothes and leave. Or something.

Her not answering me, when I asked her about that other guy, the one from the text, is grating on me. Yeah, I asked out of smugness. And yeah, unless that dude at the Farmers Market is one hell of a grower, I'm pretty sure I could answer my own question. But the fact that she didn't *say* anything...

Makes me doubt myself a little.

And I don't like that.

As I nudge the tip of my cock into her opening, Lydia starts to move her hips. She's getting impatient for me to plow into her again—which is a good sign.

"I'm going to ask you again," I say. "Has anyone ever filled you up like this?"

"No," she gasps this time.

A sheet of hair falls into her face as she turns again to look at me, and that's what does it. I can't take the tension any longer. Placing my hands on either side of her ass, I grip her soft flesh so hard she flinches and plunge my entire shaft into her until I feel myself hit her inner wall. Lydia moans. I pull out, all the way out, and catch a glimpse of my cock glistening with her wetness before I shove it back in. Her pussy molds around my cock like a sheath to a blade. I can't get enough.

Lydia reaches around to grab my hand and bring it to her chest. Her breasts are soft and full beneath my fingers, and I desperately need them both in my hands. Still pumping in and out of her, I reach around so that my chest is flush with the curve of her back, so that I'm cradling her tits in my two hands. I roll her nipples between my fingers, and she shudders.

"Will," she starts, her voice choked. "You feel so fucking good."

"Perfect," I whisper in her ear.

And I'm about to make her feel better. Because I want to see Lydia Chandler come.

I want to see her come *hard*.

Still fondling her tit in my left hand, I move my right hand to her clit and begin the circles that drove her so nuts the other day in the library.

In, out.

In, out.

All the while, circling, circling.

Never breaking rhythm.

A low whine starts in Lydia's throat. My balls are getting fucking tight now, and I don't know how much longer I can hang on without blowing my load. But I don't want to do it inside her. Even with the condom, it feels too intimate. Like something I can take back even less than whatever it is we're doing now.

But then I feel Lydia shuddering in my arms as she loses control of her hips. Her pussy spasms around my cock, and I slide out of her just in time to come while gripping the smooth skin of her ass. For a moment, the only sound is our heavy breathing, muffled by the crash of the waves on the shore. Then Lydia twists around and kisses me, and against my better judgment, I let her.

Because now, with our naked selves wrapped around each other, she feels closer than before. Like some kind of screen has gone down and she can actually see me—which is fucking scary. But for this moment, I'm choosing not to care.

As I slip the condom off and toss it into the fire, my heart rate's finally starting to settle. By the time I pull up my boxers and jeans, Lydia's already got her bra and panties back on, and she's sitting hugging herself, her skin all prickled with goosebumps.

"Hey," I say, sitting down and pulling her onto my lap.

She seems tense for a minute, like she's considering something—leaving, probably. I know I'm good at fucking, but I also know I'm shit at the rest of this stuff. Especially with her. Because no matter how good the sex is, we're still at odds. I still have to do something she'll never forgive me for—and I know something she doesn't.

Ethan called me yesterday to say the board had voted to approve the finalized plans, that they're opening things up for bids this week. He has no clue that I've ever so much as spoken to Lydia Chandler outside of the library, but even so, he made sure to mention that the board is keeping things quiet so as not to "put undue stress on employees." It doesn't take a genius to know what that means.

So when Lydia stays, nestling herself on my lap next to the fire, I'm feeling a little unsettled. If she knew the secret I was keeping, she'd be out of here in two seconds—and probably slap me in the face to boot. But I'll cross that bridge when I come to it. I'll figure out what to do.

Lydia drops her head back against my chest, and I wrap my arms around her, blocking out the wind that sweeps in off the sea. I clear my throat. There's something else I want to say to her, something a little easier. Something that, no matter how wound up it got me tonight thinking about it, I want her to know.

"I'm sorry."

Lydia cocks her head to look at me, intrigued. "For?"

"For reading that text on your phone."

She laughs softly. "That wasn't your fault. I'm the one who dropped it."

"Yeah, but I could've looked away. I saw a glimpse and I read the rest."

"Mm."

"Was it the guy from the Farmers Market?"

Lydia looks up at me. She blinks. "How'd you know?"

My arms tighten around her. "You were pretty upset to see him with somebody else—even if you tried to hide it."

"Oh." Lydia lets her head drop back on me again. Her hair smells like vanilla, sweet and somehow familiar. "Yeah. He's my ex. He started texting me again—the kind of stuff you saw. Trying to hook up, saying he wants me back. It's all bullshit, though. He's got pictures of himself with that woman on Instagram, plastered all over each other."

"Wow. Sounds like a gem."

Lydia snorts. "Yeah, he had me fooled."

I swallow hard. I can't help but think how I'm sitting here fooling her, too. The fast tracking of the library project, the family history of hurt that haunts me...

There's another reason seeing that text from Lydia's ex stuck with me. One I try not to think about, but that comes with me wherever I go, like a fucking rain cloud. I just can't shake it. It's why I've convinced myself that I'm the one who has to make sure my siblings stay on track. That they all have a roof over their heads, food in their stomachs, a shoulder to lean on.

I've never told anyone about it—not since Mom. Not since the damage was done.

But suddenly, as I'm sitting here with Lydia in my lap and her hair in my face, I want to tell her, get it off my chest. She told me about *her* parents, about losing her mom to cancer and her dad to drink. I think I could tell her about mine. I think she might actually understand.

Maybe.

"It's not the first time I saw a message I wasn't supposed to see," I say suddenly.

Lydia doesn't turn to look at me, but she strokes my arm and I know she's listening. The fire crackles beside us.

"Actually," I continue, "it was an email the first time. I don't even know if people texted back then—like, twenty-some years ago. Anyway, it was an email from my dad. To someone else. Some chick at his office. He left his email up on his work computer, and I needed to print something for school. I was only thirteen, so I don't think I really understood what I was reading. But I'd seen porn, and I wasn't an idiot, and this shit was explicit. I don't really think I believed at the time that my dad... that he could... well, *do* that. To my mom."

Lydia traces her fingers up and down my arm. "What did you do?"

"I told my mom. I forwarded the whole fucking email thread to her."

"And what did *she* do?"

"Well, she confronted my dad about it. It went about how you'd expect. Yelling. Door slamming. I don't think I ever saw my mom cry so much. And then my dad packed up —and that was it."

"Wait—what, like the next day?"

"The next day. He left his wife and four kids—and my youngest brother was three fucking months old. He just peaced on out."

Lydia's quiet for a moment, processing. "Well, fuck him."

I can't help but chuckle at the disgust in her voice. It's how I've felt every time I've thought of my dad over the past almost twenty-three years.

"Yeah," I say. "Fuck him. But also fuck me. Little old,

goody-two-shoes thirteen-year-old Will, who can't keep a fucking secret and wrecked his own family."

Lydia's fingers stop their tracing. She looks up at me, and her dark eyes are absolutely gorgeous in the firelight. "Hold up. You don't actually think that, do you?"

I shrug. "I mean... yeah. If I'd just left that shit alone, my dad would've stuck around. My mom wouldn't have had to work three jobs, my brother, Zeke, would've grown up with a dad, and I wouldn't be so fucking angry all the time."

"Will," Lydia says. "Your dad was having an affair. He might've chosen to leave regardless—you can't put that on yourself. And anyway, leaving aside that your mom would've wanted to know, *you* would have known. You would have been carrying around the same burden either way."

"Maybe. But I wouldn't be carrying around the guilt."

Lydia shakes her head, and I catch a whiff of vanilla. I want to bury my face in her hair.

"Thanks for telling me that," she says. Her voice is quiet.

"Sure," I say, because I can't think of anything else. I've never told *anyone* about that email—not even my siblings—but I have to admit it feels good. Nothing has changed, of course. The guilt and responsibility are still there. But there's a little ray of light streaming in through my darkness that wasn't there before.

We're quiet a moment, listening to the waves lapping on the shore. The fire is dying, the fading embers smoldering in the darkness. As we fold up the blanket, dust the sand off ourselves, and start our walk back into town, we keep our chatter to a minimum. I guess we're each lost in our own thoughts. Trying to figure out what the hell just happened, probably—and where the fuck we go from here.

Lydia heads home, and I hop into the cab of my truck. Her scent is still on me, mingled with mine, and although I need to shower when I get home and wash off the sweat, I almost don't want to. I want Lydia on my skin, in my arms, in my head. I want her wherever, whenever, and however I can get her. And that thought scares the absolute shit out of me.

Because, no matter how much I try to fight it, I'm still my father's son. I've got his height, his build, his blue eyes and dirty blond hair. I've got his last name, and—the worst part —I got stuck with those fucking ghosts always nagging at the edges of my mind. Shit, I'm even keeping secrets like he did now.

The Holloway blood runs through my veins, whether I like it or not. And someone like Lydia deserves a hell of a lot better than someone like me.

eighteen

Zeke's still up when I get home. He's lounging on the couch in his sweats, scrolling on his phone. There's some stupid reality show on in the background. He looks up when he hears me walk in. His blue eyes narrow deviously, and he tosses his phone aside.

"Well, you're out late," he drawls.

"Yup," I say.

I toss my jacket over the back of a chair and head to the kitchen for a Coke. The drive home with only my thoughts already has me wondering what the fuck I was thinking tonight, and I'm really not in the mood to be probed by my nosy, fuckboy little brother. It's times like this that I wish I drank—but I can't risk letting my spiritual guard down.

"I smell sex again, Will," Zeke calls from the other room, his tone taunting. "Did you finally man up and bang the librarian?"

I come back into the living room and lean against the doorway, Coke in hand. I'm clearly not going to be able to lie my way out of this one. And anyway, Zeke's assertion that it's somehow unmanly to refrain from fucking anything that moves is irritating as hell.

"Actually, yeah," I say to him, taking a swig of my soda. "I —how'd you put it?—*manned* up and banged the librarian. And you better believe I banged her better than you ever could, because I'm, you know, an *actual* man in his goddamn thirties and not a scrawny little kid."

"Oh, ho!" Zeke grins at me. He flexes his pecs, and I can just tell he's practiced that move before. "Who're you calling scrawny, bro? But seriously—*finally*. You needed that."

"Eh." I shrug. I'm not about to divulge to him just how right he was. Because what I'm afraid of is that now that I've had a taste, I'm going to *keep* needing it. Needing her. And the more I get to know Lydia, the more I understand how raw and vulnerable she is, and how badly I'm bound to hurt her.

"What? It wasn't good? I thought you said you banged her like a real man."

"Ha. It was good. It was too good."

Zeke scoffs. "Ain't no such thing. If you're getting some sweet pussy, Will, you just thank the gods and keep on gettin' it."

That makes me snort. I sometimes can't believe how carefree my youngest brother is, like he has no responsibility to anyone. I wonder, if things had been different, if I would've turned out like that. Somehow I doubt it. I've always been the responsible one. So responsible, in fact, that I even felt the need to tattle on my shitty dad and wreck our family in the process.

"Yeah, I don't think I'm going to do that," I say.

"Why? She doesn't want it?"

"I don't know."

Zeke looks aghast. "Well, make her want it! Sounds like you're off to a good start."

"I just don't think it's a good idea."

"Oh, come *on*," Zeke says, rolling his eyes. "What is it with you? She married or something?"

"Nope." I sip my Coke. "But she's really nice. Too nice for me."

"Will, seriously? Look, you're grouchy and you're kind of an asshole sometimes, but you're not a *shithead*." He suddenly narrows his eyes at me, like a thought has just occurred to him. "Oh, god. Is this about Dad again?"

"It's not about *Dad*," I snap, but I can tell my tone has already betrayed me. I just hate that two decades later, my dad is still fucking things up for me. Actually, I think *I'm* just fucked up. "It's about the fact that we're going in two different directions. I *need* to nail this library project and land that contract with Ethan Wilde so I can pay my fucking mortgage and take care of this family. Okay? And that means fucking up Lydia's dream of turning the library into a land-mark to honor her mother's memory. We can't have it both ways."

Zeke looks at me hard for a minute, then puts his hands up in mock surrender. "Okay. I get it."

"Good."

"Well, at least you got it out of your system, right?"

Zeke's eyes are back on the TV, but his mouth is twisted into his signature grin, and I know our moment has passed. I'd be lying, though, if I said I hadn't had exactly the same thought. Lydia and I got whatever this was out of our systems, and now we can get back to real life.

My phone buzzes in my pocket. I glance at the screen and my heart sinks.

> Lydia: Hey. Just wanted to make sure you got home okay.
>
> Lydia: Also, I enjoyed tonight.

Fuck.

What was I just saying about being able to get back to real life? I blow out my breath and Zeke looks up at me, his eyes questioning.

"Is that her?"

"No," I say. Because I don't want him to know what I'm about to do, which is click out of Lydia's message and shove my phone back in my pocket.

More than anything, I want to tell her that I enjoyed

tonight, too. Enjoyed it more than I've enjoyed anything in the past—god, I don't even know. It's certainly the best *sex* I've had in ages, but besides that, the fact that she allowed me to bare my body *and* past to her...

I need to stop. I've got to nip this in the bud before it goes any further. For her sake *and* mine.

I know not texting back is an asshole move, but it's better this way. I'm sure she'll be pissed at me tomorrow, but once this renovation is over and she moves on to find someone good—someone who actually knows how to love—she'll thank me for it.

nineteen

LYDIA

Will never texted back last night.

I was already on the fence about texting him. I'm trying to figure out how the hell I went from hating his guts to getting weak in the knees whenever I think about him, but somewhere along the way it happened. The damage is done. And if I'm being honest, I'd let him damage me again in a heartbeat.

The way he talked about his dad... and that email, and what happened after? It was so raw. Yes, he'd just fucked me, and yes, it was the best sex of my life, but sitting in his lap in the darkness as he told me about what happened felt a million times more intimate. His voice was so quiet but clear, like he'd been waiting his whole life to tell someone that. But that's stupid. There's no way that this man—who could clearly have any woman he wanted just by glaring down at her with those clear, sapphire eyes of his—would, for some reason only god knows, open up to *me*.

So, of course he didn't text back. I should have known.

Will hasn't been into the library since yesterday, and I can only imagine what that means. He's probably sitting with his feet up on an office desk, perfecting those freaking blueprints. Even with the redesigned foyer, I know it's not going to be enough. The requirements for securing landmark status are clear, and unless I can talk Will—and the board—into turning the downstairs meeting room into a computer lab, my dream is gone.

But I'm still holding out hope. Contrary to what I first thought, Will is a decent guy. Once the awkwardness dies down, I'm going to try one more time to make my case— even if it means getting on my knees and begging. Because now that I think about it, why *can't* the downstairs meeting room be turned into a computer lab? It'd save the city money, preserve the authenticity of the floor plan, and probably even get the project done faster.

Hell, that sounds like a win-win for everyone... right?

"How's it going out here, Lydia?"

I'm snapped out of my thoughts as Nancy comes striding out of her office. I paste on a smile. "Going fine, thanks."

"I'm stepping out for a coffee run. You want anything?"

I shake my head. I'm jittery enough the way it is, my mind constantly running through plausible floor plan options I could push for with Will... which then makes me remember how warm his mouth was between my legs. Another coffee is going to send me through the absolute roof. But I'm certainly not going to tell Nancy that.

"Okay," Nancy says. "Suit yourself. Say, has Will been by today?"

"Not that I've seen," I say, shrugging.

Nancy looks at me like she's about to say something, but then thinks better of it. I wonder suddenly what she would think if she knew that I'd come all over Will Holloway's fingers in the next room over. There better not be fucking cameras in this place.

"Well, if you see him, tell him that Ethan Wilde wants to know—"

"What's Ethan Wilde want to know?"

Will comes thundering up the foyer steps, and I hear the front door swing closed behind him. As he strides into the main room, removing his sunglasses and hanging them from the unbuttoned collar of his flannel shirt, he gazes around the room, squinting up at the windows.

"Oh, *great* timing," Nancy chirps, like she's just delighted beyond belief to see him. And honestly, if he hadn't completely ignored me last night after fucking me and talking to me like it meant something, I might be happy to see him, too.

But he *did* ignore me. And I am *not* happy to see him. So when his gaze moves to mine and lingers there, I keep my face neutral. Like nothing between us ever happened. I mean, that's what he wants—right?

"Yeah, gotta check some lighting stuff," Will says, breaking eye contact with me and flashing a smile at Nancy. "Can I help with something?"

As Nancy explains to Will what Ethan Wilde wants to know—something about hardware and what fixtures Will plans to use—I try hard not to look at him, to play it cool. For all he knows, I haven't even noticed he didn't text me back. But once or twice I feel his gaze flick over to me, and it takes every single ounce of my strength not to look up at him.

When Nancy finally leaves for Brewed Awakening, Will swaggers over to me and hoists himself onto my desk. He raps his knuckles on the desk in front of me.

"Hey."

"Get off my desk," I say.

"Make me."

I look up at him. "Are you kidding me right now?"

"Not in the slightest."

"Will, I'm working. I've got actual shit to do."

"Me, too."

"Okay, so get to it. Don't you have to check—" I gesture vaguely. "—lighting stuff?"

"I will. I just want to talk. About last night."

"Oh, *now* you want to talk?" I lay down my pencil with more force than I mean to, fully aware that I've just blown my cover. He now *definitely* knows I'm pissed about the text—or lack thereof.

Will winces. He grins sheepishly. "Sorry, I was tired. You can't fault me for that."

"I don't fault you for anything."

I go back to scanning barcodes. I've got a lot of books to shelve, so if Will's got a point to make, I hope he gets to it fast. I'm also not sure how long I can keep up the aloof act with that spicy pine scent of his drifting toward me from across the desk. He smells so damn good.

"Huh." Will stares at me for another moment, then looks to the ceiling, like he's pondering something. "Well, tomorrow will be interesting. With you not talking to me, seems like that'll be a pretty shit booth we're running. Damn shame for the library."

Well, shit.

He's right. The fall festival is tomorrow afternoon. We've got to man that stupid fundraiser booth—which I'm not happy about, anyway. But I couldn't say no to helping the library with *fundraising*.

I draw in a deep breath through my nose, but I don't turn to look at him. It's what he wants, and I won't let him get to me.

"I'm sure we'll figure it out," I say, my tone crisp.

"Right." Will's quiet a moment before he hops off the desk. I can tell he wants to say something else, but, like me, is holding back. "Well, I guess I'll get back to work."

"You do that."

I steal a glance up at him, and he's looking at me like I just slammed a door in his face for no reason. I feel a little guilty. After all, I went into last night with eyes wide open. I knew perfectly well we were at odds, and that Will's goals are in direct conflict with mine. I'm also aware that just because someone fucks you, it doesn't mean they want anything further with you. So I really don't have a reason to be pissed at him.

As Will heads back to the foyer, still squinting up at the windows and tapping furiously into his phone, I realize what my problem is. I don't even think I'm pissed at Will at all. I think I'm pissed at myself for thinking anything could ever change.

twenty

WILL

Zeke: Can ghosts have, like, venereal diseases?

Phoebe: I'm surprised you can use that word in a sentence. But no. I don't think so.

Zeke: Ok. Anyway, where's Will?

Benji: This is the  group chat

Will: Holy duck. I'm volunteering at the fall festival all afternoon.

Will: *Duck

Will: *Duck!!

Will: F-U-C-K

The weather is gorgeous on Saturday afternoon as I come rolling down Main Street and whip my truck into a parking spot off one of the side roads. The sky is clear and blue, and the sun's shining overhead, but there's a chilly little bite in the air that reminds you it's autumn. We really couldn't have asked for better weather for the fall crafts festival today. People are sure to be out and about, enjoying the sunshine.

"Will! Over here!"

I step down from the truck and scan the square to see who's calling me. The place isn't crowded yet, and it only takes a quick glance before I see Nancy, waving excitedly from behind the table she's already set up on the sidewalk. Beside her, Lydia's unloading something from a huge box on the table. She looks up at me briefly, then goes back to her work without so much as a wave. I guess the weather isn't raising her spirits this afternoon like it is mine.

Well, that's just fine. We're not besties. Hell, we're not even *friends*. We're two people who gave into our primal urges, had a good time doing so, and are now going our separate ways. End of story. Except I still need to tell her about that final approval from the board.

God.

I shove the thought from my mind and head over to the booth. "Lovely day out today, isn't it?"

"Oh, just *glorious*," Nancy gushes. She claps her hands together and gazes in wonder at the spread of other tables being set up in the square. "Hopefully we get a good turnout."

Lydia lifts her now empty box from the table and flattens it, setting it down below and out of the way. She turns her attention to the brown paper bundles heaped on the table in front of her, starts sorting them into groups and lining them up.

"So what have we got today, exactly?" I venture, nodding to the packages. I know it's some kind of book sale, but no one's told me anything further than that. I'm just here as the architect, the face of the project. The board thought it'd be helpful if people could come by and ask me questions directly about the details of the renovation.

"Blind date with a book," Lydia says, still not looking up.

"Okay..."

Nancy clucks her tongue, and Lydia sighs, finally sparing me a glance while she continues her work. I'm honestly surprised to see a little patch of color rising in her cheeks. She chews her lip as she talks, looking suddenly shy.

"I wrapped the books in brown paper so no one will see the titles. But they've got these cards on the front that give you a few details about the vibe of the book, who the characters may be—that kind of thing."

"Huh." I pick up one of the wrapped books and scan the handwritten card stuck to the front. "Spooky. Main character is a little boy. Do not read while snowed in."

"The Shining," Lydia says. There's a small smile on her lips. "Stephen King."

That gets a chuckle out of me. I place the book back on the table and Lydia swipes it away, adding it to her lineup.

"The books are five dollars apiece," Nancy says. She's got a wad of bills fanned out in front of her and is counting through them. "But obviously, it's a fundraiser, so people are welcome to donate more if they'd like. I suspect we'll get a number who'd like to contribute checks, too."

Lydia gives the rows of books one last little shuffle, making sure they're all lying perfectly arranged, the cards visible beneath the red and white string she's tied in a bow around each of them. It really looks like a table covered in old-fashioned Christmas presents.

She steps back from the table, flipping her long dark hair over her shoulder. The delicious vanilla scent that wafts toward me is tempting as shit, and I've got the sudden urge to let my mind go in places it shouldn't right now. This is a family event. Sporting a boner from behind this table would be one thousand percent unacceptable.

"There," Lydia announces.

She looks at Nancy, pointing out the groupings of books on the table. "Left side is adult fiction, the middle is young adult, and on the right we've got kids. *Magic Treehouse*, that sort of thing. And with that, I'm going to get coffee. Be back in a few."

Lydia scoops up her purse from behind the table, turns on her heel, and strides briskly off across the square. I've got half a mind to call after her and ask if she'll bring me a dark roast, but Nancy didn't ask for anything and I don't want to risk waking Lydia's wrath this morning. Besides, she's already halfway down the street.

"Lydia's coming around," Nancy remarks.

She plops herself in a folding chair behind the table and looks up at me through her sunglasses. "I figure I'll wait until the official announcement to tell her the finalized plans are approved and the bids are going, but I think she's making peace with the whole thing."

"You think?" I ask. More cars are pulling up, and the square's slowly beginning to crowd with more people.

"Oh, definitely." Nancy waves a hand. "She's barely mentioned a word to me this past week."

I'm not surprised Lydia hasn't said anything else to Nancy. She probably figures Nancy's a lost cause—and doesn't hold any real power over the situation, anyway. No, if Lydia wanted to change the course of the renovation, she'd go to someone who holds some sway.

And she has. Ahem.

"Well, that's good. I was thinking, though, that maybe I ought to tell her about the bidding."

"You?" Nancy looks surprised.

I shrug. "Yeah. I'm the one in the know, I guess. She'll probably want details."

Nancy chuckles. "That may be so, but I'd come wearing a suit of armor for that conversation, if I were you. Don't take this the wrong way, but... let's just say she's not your biggest fan."

"I'm aware."

Our conversation is cut short by a couple of women who come up to the table and greet Nancy with shrieks and hugs. I may live in Hawthorne Bay, but I like my distance and hate small talk, so I smile politely and settle back onto one of the folding chairs. Nancy doesn't even notice. She's gesturing to the book bundles, explaining the blind date concept to the women. If they want to ask about the blueprints for the building, they can have at it. I'm in plain sight.

As Nancy talks, I look around the square, enjoying the nip of the air on my face and taking in the sights. The little downtown square of Hawthorne Bay is littered with booths, and people stroll leisurely between shops, stopping to admire the window displays strung up with brightly colored leaves and spread with piles of pumpkins. I'm pretty sure I can smell cinnamon rolls, most likely coming from one of the booths.

"Here." Lydia appears at my elbow and thrusts a paper cup toward me.

I frown. I'm not her freaking purse. She can set her coffee down on the table while she takes her coat off—*oh*. She's holding two coffees, one in each hand, and carefully avoiding my gaze. I take the one she's holding out to me, deliberately letting my fingers brush hers as I do. Her skin is warm, and so is the coffee.

"This is... for me?" I ask.

"Yeah."

"What is it?"

"Drip coffee. Dark roast."

I take a sip, and it's dark roast indeed. There's no sugar, no milk. It's exactly the way I like it.

"Thanks," I say. "You didn't need to do that."

Lydia shrugs. I think I catch the tiniest of smiles from her before she turns back to the table and joins the conversation Nancy's having with the small group of people now sifting through the blind date books. Lydia asks them what they're in the mood for, and, when the answer is historical romance, she rifles through the rows of bundles and extracts a few different options. As the would-be readers peruse their choices, discussing among themselves, I can't take my eyes off Lydia. She's so polished, so poised. And apparently also well read, which isn't much of a surprise given her choice of career.

But underneath that polished exterior, I know there's a whole other side to this woman smoldering beneath the surface. She's like magma, Lydia is. Hot and roiling and fierce. Uncontainable. She's a fucking force of nature, and I don't even think she knows it. The way she hasn't backed down about this damn library, always looking me straight in the eye as she plows ahead with her opinion, whether or not it's going to cost her. How she looked the other night, gazing back at me with sparks in her eyes, down on all fours in front of me on the sand...

Fuck. Don't go there, Will. This is a fundraiser, not a dick-raiser.

I move my eyes back to the square, trying to steer my mind back into reality. Across the way, there's the cinnamon roll booth, and next to it is a table covered with candles and handmade soaps. I sip my coffee, relishing the warmth of the paper cup on my cold hands.

There's a guy at the candle booth perusing the bars of soap who looks kind of familiar. He's got on a ball cap, and the jacket and jeans he's wearing look absolutely pristine, like he ironed them before leaving the house or something. I'm about to give up on trying to place the guy when he lifts his cap to run a hand over a thatch of smooth, perfectly coiffed hair—and it hits me.

Well, well, well. If it isn't Mr. Mediocre Lay himself.

It's all I can do to keep a smirk off my face as I study the guy from afar, watching as he moves on to sniffing candles. He's alone this time, which either means the blonde slept in, or they're not the item Lydia thought they were. *Or* he's here because he knows Lydia will be, and from the way he keeps glancing over here, I'd be willing to bet that's exactly what it is. He's here to make his move.

Poor guy doesn't know I already made mine.

When the guy looks up from the candles and zeroes in on our table, I stand up from my folding chair, moving nonchalantly to stand by Lydia as Nancy chats with another passerby. From the corner of my eye, I can see him making his way toward our booth, but I busy myself with one of the book parcels, studying the card on the front: *Romance. Regency. Downton Abbey, but make it spicy.*

I have no fucking clue.

"Hey, Lyds."

I can tell by the way Lydia bristles next to me that she hadn't seen the guy approaching. But she keeps her cool, always poised and collected, greeting him in an even voice that betrays nothing. "Dylan. How's it going?"

The guy dips his hands in his jeans pockets. "Oh, not bad at all. Beautiful day."

"Mmhm."

Dylan rifles through the books, and I honestly wonder if this guy's ever read an entire book before. It's pretty clear from the way he's flipping through them he's not even reading the cards on the front.

"So..." the douche drawls. "You got plans tonight? My entire weekend's clear, and I thought we could... pick up where we left off."

Seriously? Nancy's still chatting with a visitor, but I'm standing right here—flipping through a brochure about the renovation, yet clearly listening. But Dylan's looking up at Lydia with a gross, sultry sort of half smile on his face, and I'm pretty sure my presence hasn't even registered.

Lydia barely even reacts, just straightens the packages that Dylan's been digging through. She plucks the one he's holding right out of his hands and places it on the top of the pile.

"Nah. No thanks," she says.

"Aw, really?" Dylan's tone is whining. "I've got that pizza oven, we could—"

I cut him off. "She said no."

Next to me, I feel Lydia stiffen. For a split second, her eyes flit to mine, and then they're back on the books she's straightening that are already sufficiently straight.

Dylan shoots a grin at me, which is more like a flash of bared teeth. "Hey, uh. Hi. Do we know each other? Or...?"

"We haven't met, if that's what you're asking," I say. I give him a curt nod. "Will Holloway."

Dylan runs his tongue along his top teeth, studying me. His eyes flick to the brochures fanned out on the table, and he nods, realization dawning. "Holloway, huh? You're the architect."

"That's me."

I cross my arms over my chest, watch Dylan set his jaw as he sizes me up. Although there's no doubt this guy is fit— probably shoots hoops on the weekends or something—my arms are easily twice the size of his. Like, come on, bro. Do you even *lift*?

Lydia, who's clearly picked up on this silent standoff, sighs. "Are you buying a book, Dylan? It's for the fundraiser. Blind date with a book."

"Interesting," Dylan says, his attention back on Lydia. He studies the books in front of him."How's it work? Someone buys a book—and they get to go on a blind date with you?"

He laughs, and I can tell he actually thinks his joke is funny.

"Not exactly," Lydia says.

She gives him a pitying kind of smile, but doesn't take the bait, just explains the concept to him the same way she's explained it to every other visitor.

"Well, you got any recommendations?" Dylan asks, now fingering the books in a way that makes me want to puke.

Lydia shrugs. "Depends what you're in the mood for."

Dylan looks straight at her, ignoring me. "What about something naughty?"

My blood goes cold. Is he for fucking real? Lydia's blushing, clearing her throat, stammering something about how that's not really appropriate, how maybe she ought to pass him off to Nancy. He says he's kidding, that it was just a joke.

But when he reaches out and starts stroking her arm, I see fucking red.

Now I'm pissed.

I don't know who this guy thinks he is, showing up every place Lydia goes and yanking her chain, all while spending the other days of the week with another woman he flaunts on social media. This guy is messed up—and he's sorely mistaken.

Lydia Chandler is *not* a side piece. Lydia Chandler is the

main fucking deal. And if this guy's too stupid to realize that, I'm more than happy to spell it out for him.

"I've got a recommendation," I say. I move to the other side of the table and start digging through the titles Lydia said were children's books. I draw one out, present it totally straight-faced to Dylan. "Here. This one. *Magic. Mummies. To go back in time, two friends need look no further than their back-yard.* Trust me, this one's a gem."

Dylan only looks at the book, clearly doubtful but trying to play it cool. "I don't know if that sounds like my kind of thing..."

I unwrap the parcel, surprised but glad when Lydia says nothing. I glance at the cover, trying to keep my lips from twitching, and hold it up to Dylan with a huge, opened-mouth grin of faux amazement.

"Oh, my god. Look at that—Magic Treehouse! Mummies in the goddamn morning. I know it'll take you a while to get through, but you're in for a treat."

Beside me, Lydia stifles a snort. Dylan's lip curls and he huffs out a breath. "Wow, real mature, man."

I nod solemnly. "I know. It is. I didn't read Magic Tree-house until I was nine, but I think you can handle it. I have faith in you."

"Dude. What's your problem?" Dylan's neck is red. I can tell it's taking everything he has not to snarl at me, and I absolutely love it.

I keep my face light, my expression stoic, as I plant my palms on the table and lean toward him. "I'll tell you what my problem is, Dylan. My problem is that Lydia *told you no.* And if you think that's your invitation to just try harder, then

I better find you another book—because you're even more of a child than I thought."

Dylan snorts, like he can't believe I just said that to him. Lydia sighs, flicks her hand at the two of us, and goes to join Nancy, who's still chatting obliviously away with a group of visitors. I keep my eyes trained on Dylan. I'm not kidding around here.

"Whatever, man," Dylan says, scowling. "You've got issues."

"Sure do. And you're one of them. Now get walking."

When he shoves his hands in his pockets and finally turns to go, stalking across the street without a single look behind him, I chance a glance at Lydia. She's still talking with Nancy, sifting through the books, but she catches my look and gives me a roll of her dark eyes.

I'm really hoping I didn't overstep and piss Lydia off— that she's not going to accuse me of trying to play the hero again. But I was sick of watching that dickbag slink around, trying to get back what he gave up.

Because... god. Lydia can do so much better.

twenty-one

WILL

The market picks up from there, and there's almost always a cluster of visitors around our table. Lydia's blind date books are a big hit, and we get a lot of folks asking questions about the renovation plans. Whenever someone picks up a brochure, Lydia's careful to busy herself with the books, not wanting to appear too interested in any of the questions they ask me.

And, for my part, I'm careful not to say anything too concrete about timelines. I'm still trying to figure out the best time and way to tell Lydia that the board approved my finalized blueprints, and that time is most definitely *not* in front of a bunch of people at the Hawthorne Bay fall market. I'm going to have to tell her soon, though. I'm starting to feel downright dishonest.

As the sun sets and the chill of the evening starts to creep in, the groups of people milling around thin out. We've sold most of the books Lydia wrapped, and although they haven't counted the donations yet, quite a few people have been giving more than the suggested five dollars. That's a good sign.

Nancy glances at her watch, then nudges Lydia. "Hey. I told you we'd go 'til seven. If you want to head out, I can take it from here. There's not much to pack up."

"Really?" Lydia looks dubious.

Nancy waves a hand. "Yes, yes, yes. Plenty of people around to help me load up the table and chairs. Books will be a cinch."

"Okay..."

"You too, Will," Nancy says. She flicks her hand at me, beaming. "Enjoy the evening."

Lydia gives Nancy's arm a little squeeze, then grabs her purse and gives us a wave. Almost before I even realize it, she's taking off down the sidewalk, and I have to mutter a quick goodbye to Nancy so I can catch up.

As I fall into step beside her, Lydia turns to glance at me. I'm still worried she's pissed at me about Dylan, but right now she just looks resigned. "What?"

"I need to talk to you about something. Can I walk with you?"

Lydia sniffs. "Looks like you already are."

"Are you pissed about Dylan? He deserved it, you know."

"He did." The corners of Lydia's mouth quiver, and I can tell she's holding back a smile. That, at least, is a relief. "Is that what you jogged over here to say?"

"No." I take a deep breath, then just come out with it. "The finalized plans are approved."

"I know," Lydia says. She doesn't look my way.

"You do? Nancy told you?"

"What are you talking about? I was there at the stake-holder meeting."

I shake my head. "No, I mean... *approved* approved. Like, done. We've started the bidding."

Lydia stops walking. The wind has blown her long hair across her face, and she shoves it aside. "Wait—so that's it? There's nothing you can do to stop it now?"

Well, this is awkward.

"I mean... I could, I guess, in theory... but no. It's progressing."

Lydia goes completely stone-faced. I can almost feel the adrenaline rush through her body as she processes the news and what it means for any hope she might've had left. Although surely by now she *must* know I'm not going to magically give up a career-changing project, nor is the board going to magically change its mind about the renovation. They *voted* on it, for Christ's sake.

If Lydia was going to say something, she's thought better of it. She starts walking again, faster now, and I can't tell if she's about to burst into tears and wants to make it home before that, or if she's trying to outpace me, leaving me behind in a flurry of fallen leaves.

"Lydia."

I'm jogging to keep up with her, but she doesn't answer. She just rounds the corner, looks both ways, and crosses to the other side of the street. I realize I have no idea where she's going, but I follow her anyway, coming to a stop behind her as she pulls up onto the front stoop of a cute little house a few blocks away.

She glares back over her shoulder as she unlocks the door. "Why are you still here?"

"You're pissed, and I don't like it."

Lydia snorts. "Ha. *You* don't like it."

"That's right. I don't like it when someone who doesn't deserve to be hurt gets hurt. And don't even try to tell me you're not—it's written all over you. I think we... got caught up in stuff. I just wanted to sort it out with you, make sure everyone's on the same page."

Lydia throws her hands in the air helplessly. She pushes the door open and steps inside, not bothering to close it, which I take to mean she's okay with me following her. Or at least not going to, like, pull a knife on me.

As I close the front door softly behind me, my phone buzzes in my pocket. It's the second time in the last ten minutes, but whoever it is can wait. This conversation is important, and I need to stay focused, present.

Lydia's already made her way through the entryway to the kitchen and is filling up a glass of water from the fridge. Her house is simple, one of those minimalist motifs, with tiny pops of color here and there. It's really homey, which is honestly no surprise. It fits her somehow.

Lydia leans back against the counter, dark eyes glaring at me as she sips her water. Her hair is tangled from the wind, but it's as beautiful as it's ever been, and I'm trying really fucking hard not to think about pulling it. Or what we were doing while I pulled it the other night. Or where my dick was.

Fuck.

Focus, Will.

I pull out a barstool at the counter and sink down onto it. Lydia just eyes me, but she doesn't tell me to get up. I clear my throat.

"So you only just found out the plans are approved?" Lydia's eyes are boring holes into my skull.

"I've known since Monday," I admit. I don't like where this is going.

"You've known since Monday," Lydia repeats. She's got the snide look of someone who's predicted something terrible would happen and has just been proven right. "So, you're saying you knew about this the other night? The other night when—when we..."

Well, shit. I've got only myself to blame here. I should have expected this.

"Yes. I'm sorry."

Lydia scoffs, holding my gaze. As she moseys across the kitchen to me, coming to stand in front of where I'm sitting, I realize my heart is racing. Honestly, I don't think I've ever seen a ghost who looks as goddamn scary as Lydia does at this moment.

"Okay. Let me put this another way. You had this knowledge when you decided it would be a good idea to fuck me? Next to the fucking beach?"

Shit. This is not good.

I chew my lip for a moment, thinking of how the hell I'm going to get out of this one. But hearing Lydia talk about last night, hearing her say aloud that I fucked her, is hot as hell. And my cock is not getting the message that this moment is *not* a good one to get hard. Down, boy. *Down.*

"Yes," I mutter. I break eye contact, trying to concentrate

on anything but Lydia's full lips. My dick's still stiffening in my jeans, and I shift slightly on the stool to try to make it less noticeable.

But it doesn't work. Lydia's eyes flash to my junk. She sniffs, eyes narrowing.

"Are you kidding me, Will? Are you seriously getting hard while we're having this conversation?"

"Yes. No. I mean, I can't help it. Ignore it."

Good god. What the fuck was I thinking, coming here? This was not a good plan.

"Ignore it?! Have *you* ever tried to have a serious conversation with someone who's got a fucking zucchini pressed up against their pant leg?"

I can't help but chuckle at that, and I'm relieved when the corners of her lips pull up, too.

"Can't say that I have," I concede. "I imagine it must be terribly distracting."

"It is," she says.

Her eyes trace the outline of my cock, which gives an involuntary twitch as I realize what it is she's looking at. I close my eyes. My heart's starting to race again, but I did *not* come here to fuck things up further. I came here to set things straight, to get us out of this mess we somehow got ourselves into. I have one job only, and that job is to—

Oh, fuck.

When I open my eyes, Lydia's moved closer. She's standing between my legs, and her fingers are already moving toward the button of my jeans.

"Hey, hey, hey," I murmur. I need to get her attention before she starts something in motion that we're both going to regret. As though that's even an option anymore. "Are you sure this is a good idea?"

"We are *so* far past good ideas, Will. We both know this is a terrible idea, but we both know we don't care."

I swallow hard as Lydia unzips me. "Don't we?"

"Stop talking," Lydia says. "If you want to do something for me, just stop talking."

That shuts me up. How could it not? She's down on her knees now, tugging my jeans and boxers down, letting my cock spring up between us, and there's no way I'm going to stop her. For what? So I can make some lame little speech about how we need to stop whatever this is because it's only going to end badly?

I don't *want* to stop whatever this is. Not when she's got her fingers wrapped around my shaft. What, so I'm not going to say no to a blow job or whatever it is she's planning to do here? Sue me. We'll figure it out later.

Lydia presses her lips to the tip of my cock, and I hiss involuntarily. She looks up at me from under dark, fringing lashes, and she's so fucking pretty I think I might melt. "Can I?"

I nod. She's got to be crazy if she thinks I'm going to tell her no.

"Good."

Lydia bends her head again and starts licking down the side of my cock. It's been a while since anyone's sucked me off, and the warmth and wetness of her mouth on my skin is enough to make me shudder. If Lydia notices, she doesn't show it, just keeps on with her tongue, licking and sucking around my shaft. It already feels so fucking good, and I'm barely even in her mouth yet.

Lydia runs her cheek against the length of my cock. "You're so smooth."

I give a shaky laugh, not trusting myself to speak. I don't know what words are going to come out if I do, or if my voice will even hold. Instead, my fingers find the curve of her jaw as I guide her face toward the tip. I want to be completely inside her mouth.

For a moment, Lydia complies. She licks along the seam of my tip, swirling her tongue against the head, about driving me mad as she does. It's all I can do not to grab her head and force myself down her throat as I groan with pleasure.

"Fuck, Lydia. Your mouth is so warm. So wet."

Seeing her look up at me while on her knees, the head of my cock between her soft, pillowy lips, is like a wet dream come to life. My dick is rock hard, and my balls are so tight I feel like I'm going to burst. Actually, I'd like to. All over her gorgeous face.

There's a buzzing noise, and we both tense. It's my damn phone, vibrating again in the pocket of my jeans. Lydia looks at me questioningly, clearly wondering whether I want her to stop so I can answer it. I dig the phone out of my pocket, silence it, and toss it onto the counter.

"Ignore it," I say. "For the love of god, ignore it."

And then every thought I had flies straight out of my head as Lydia absolutely does ignore my buzzing phone and instead takes my entire length into her mouth and sucks. Hard.

"Holy shit," I groan. "Sweet mother of... fuck."

I can feel the warm vibrations of Lydia's laugh around my cock. She's sliding her mouth up and down my shaft now, sucking so hard her cheeks are hollowed and I'm afraid for a second I might blow my load before I've even had time to enjoy this.

"Lydia," I grind out. "It's... a good thing... you've got such a big fucking mouth."

Again, I feel the warmth of her laugh on my dick. Her hair's falling around her face as she bobs up and down on me, and suddenly, I can't resist anymore. Before I even realize it, I'm gripping her silky hair in my fist and pulling, pulling, so her head tilts all the way back and my cock slides out of her mouth.

"It's a good thing," I continue, my fingers still gripping her hair. "Because you're going to need that big mouth of yours for what I'm about to do. And I suspect you'll be a lot less mouthy while I'm doing it."

We lock eyes, and although there's something in hers that looks uncertain, there's also a challenge. She smiles slightly, leaning forward to wrap her parted lips around my head and start engulfing me with her sweet, wet mouth.

And then I take it from there. I stand up from the barstool and thrust my hips forward, ramming myself all the way to the back of her throat. She gags, but she doesn't shy away. Instead, she grips my ass and pulls me closer, taking me so far down her throat it makes my thighs shake. When she moans, I know she's into it, and I grip the hair of her scalp, pulling hard to tug her up and down my shaft as I thrust.

It's fucking heaven. And something feral inside me unleashes.

"Lydia," I growl, still gripping the back of her head. "You're going to swallow."

She nods, but it's not a request. It's a fucking order.

Because I need it. This beautiful woman kneeling below me has been inching her way ever closer to the parts of me I can't let anyone see—and it's fucking terrifying. I can almost *feel* myself losing control, feel my guards dropping every time she flashes that coy little smile. This is my last desperate grasp at control.

I pull Lydia's head in toward me and let myself go. The wave of release that floods through me as my dick stills, and then jerks, emptying into her mouth while she looks up at me and swallows down every last bit of my cum, is absolutely shattering. For a minute, I'm not sure my knees are going to hold me up, but they do, and I stroke Lydia's hair gently as she slides me out of her mouth. She presses a kiss to my tip, and I fall back, bare-assed, onto the barstool.

I lean back, flinging my forearm across my face. "Jesus Christ, woman."

Lydia laughs softly. "Just repaying the favor. From the other day..."

I let my arm drop and look at her. "Oh, we're keeping score now?"

She shrugs. "You did me a favor last week, and then we both benefitted the other night. That leaves you the odd one out. So, there you go."

The idea that she's just repaying me for when I finger fucked her against the wall brings a flash of disappointment.

I push it away, focusing instead on the wave of relief it also brings. Maybe that's all this is: settling the score. I should be happy about that.

"Well, I guess we're even now," I say, zipping myself up.

"Guess so," Lydia says. "Glad we're square."

"Alright, so…" I stand, running a hand aimlessly through my hair. My thighs are still quivering, and I'm having a hard time gathering my thoughts. What the fuck did I even *come* here for? Now, in the aftermath of that glorious blowjob, I can't even begin to imagine how I thought this would be a good idea. I need to get my head screwed on straight. "Where's the bathroom?"

Lydia tips her head to the hallway, and I head off in that direction. I just need to be away from her for a few minutes. Take a few breaths, try to get my shit together. I'm already feeling guilty for letting Lydia suck me off, and I need to figure out how to handle it. Even if it *was* transactional like she claims, I'm pretty sure she won't be thrilled once she knows I've already sent Ethan my recommendations for contractors. I didn't manage to get to *that* part.

There's also the problem that I *like* having Lydia's mouth wrapped around my cock. And the way I'm feeling right now, I'd probably kill someone to have her do that again. As I stare at my reflection in Lydia's bathroom mirror, I just want to bang my stupid head against it. I can't stay away from the woman whose childhood memories I will now officially be wrecking—and I haven't even told her everything I know. I'm fucking weak.

While we were manning the blind date book booth, I sent Ethan the names of a few of the contractors I've worked with in the past, and now I'm wishing I would've waited. Ethan doesn't pussyfoot around. Although the bulk of construction won't happen until the spring, he's itching to get the foundation for the new computer lab poured before winter, and he's certainly not going to slow things down for the assistant librarian. God.

I'd still been planning to tell Lydia today, but now that I'm here—with my dick freshly blown, no less—I don't think I can handle having to traipse back out there and tell the woman who just got on her knees for me that there's more to the bits I told her on the way here.

Jesus, Mary, and *fucking* Joseph. I've really fucked us both.

I splash some water on my face, then search my pockets for my phone. Maybe I can... do some kind of damage control. Come up with a reason to get the board to hold off on the groundbreaking a little longer. I need to text Ethan, buy myself a little more time with Lydia.

But my phone's not there. Where the hell is it?

And then I remember. It's on the counter. Shit, shit, shit.

Without even bothering to wipe my still wet hands on the towel, I hurl myself out the door and make my way down the hall, praying the whole way that Lydia won't have seen anything I don't want her to see yet.

All I wanted to do after Will came in my mouth and I'd swallowed him down was stand up and kiss the hell out of him. He looked so undone, sitting sprawled back on my kitchen barstool, his pants unzipped and his cock absolutely finished, that I couldn't take my eyes off him. Knowing I'd made him look like that—and feel that good—was exhilarating.

But I didn't kiss him. There was something in the wary way he looked at me as he zipped himself up that told me I'd be crossing some kind of line. Which is wild, given all the lines we've crossed these past couple weeks. I kind of figured… what's one more? But he's right. I may not hate his guts like I used to, but there's still the fact that he's the contractor on that fucking renovation project. We've got to draw the line somewhere. Then again, they haven't started work on the computer lab yet. I'm still hoping…

Will's phone is buzzing again where he left it on the counter. I glance over at it, shrugging off the vague notion that I probably shouldn't violate his privacy. But it's *there*. And it's loud. And it's vibrating so hard it's dancing all over the damn counter. So I swipe it up.

And my body goes cold.

It's Ethan Wilde, and I realize pretty fucking fast what the text is about. And although I don't know Will's password, enough of the text has come up on the preview screen that it's instantly clear: Will has been anything but honest.

From: Ethan Wilde

Great! Reached out to your first rec, calling for bids starting Monday! Thanks for facilitating.

The text cuts off. As a chilling rage begins to creep over me, I suddenly realize that these plans are way further along than anyone bothered to tell me.

And Will knew. He fucking *knew*.

When I look up, Will's in the doorway. His face is solemn. Clearly, he's sobered up from the high of the head I just gave him. He just looks at me, sighs, and holds out his hand for his phone.

I don't give it to him right away. Instead, I hold it up so the preview screen flashes again, and Ethan Wilde's text appears across the screen. "Were you ever going to tell me about this? Or were you just going to wait until everything happened and I had no choice but to find out?"

He doesn't say anything, just reaches for the phone.

I pull it out of his reach. "Will Holloway, you answer me right now."

Will sighs. He runs a hand through his hair, giving up on the phone for the moment. "I was going to tell you. I was figuring out how."

"Oh, how *convenient*," I snarl. "I guess you reasoned that once you told me there'd be no more fucking in the firelight, no more blowjobs on the kitchen floor, huh?"

"Lydia, it's not like that—"

"Spare me the bullshit, Will. I'm not that dumb."

"I don't think you're dumb."

"Well, it sure seems like you do, because you really fucking played me."

He stares at me for what feels like forever. Then, plucking his phone from my unsuspecting grip, he steps around me and grabs his wallet and keys off the kitchen counter.

"We've got to stop this," he says as he shoves his keys into his pocket. "I don't think you're dumb, and I didn't mean for you to get hurt. But we've got to stop now before it goes any further."

He doesn't have to say *what* we're stopping. I know.

"I couldn't agree more. Consider it stopped."

"Okay." He stops at the door. "Look, I'll see you around, alright? And whatever you want to know about the renovation specs or where the project goes from here, I'm an open book."

I don't bother to say goodbye as I shut the door after him. I feel cheap, used. Even if he meant what he said about not meaning for me to get hurt, he did a really shitty job of avoiding it. But mainly, I'm mad at myself. I should have known better than to put myself in this position again, to give someone else the chance to leave me behind in the dust. Because that's what's always going to happen. They will always choose someone—some*thing*—over me.

Will may not think I'm dumb, but I sure do.

twenty-three

WILL

I hardly even remember the walk from Lydia's house back to where my truck's parked at the library, and it's not until I'm sitting safely in the cab that I dare to open Ethan's text. I didn't even catch a glimpse of the text preview as Lydia was waving my phone around, but I could tell from her face that she'd seen enough to know what's going on.

I've got a ton of missed calls that I don't even glance at

and a bunch of texts from Zeke, but I'll get to them later. Right now, I need to see what Ethan said.

> Ethan: Great! Reached out to your first rec and got a bid! Thanks for facilitating. I want to get the groundbreaking in before first frost—maybe next week?

When I read Ethan's text, I let my head fall back against the headrest. It's pretty incriminating. If she's already reacting the way she did when she doesn't even know we're going to have to take those two main walls out, I'm not even going to bother telling her. It's a hassle I don't need, and it'll only make it worse for her. I've got a job to do, and what I need to do now is just fucking do it.

I put the truck in gear and head out. I'm hoping to god that Zeke's not home when I get there, because if I have to hear him sniff the air and say I smell like sex I just might punch him in his perfect little face. Then again, going home to an empty house seems pretty damn lonely, too. But I guess that's par for the course for me, isn't it? I've always known I'd be better off alone, staying out of everyone else's business and keeping them out of mine. Better for everyone else, too.

I'm pulling into my driveway when a call comes over the speakers: *Phoebe Holloway*.

I groan, but I answer it anyway. If Phoebe needs one of her brothers, she almost always calls Benji—because, I mean, he's her twin. She doesn't usually call me, so I'm hoping everything's okay.

"What's up?"

"Where are you?" Phoebe's voice is tense.

"Driving."

"Okay, well..." Phoebe pauses. "I don't know how to say this exactly, but... Zeke's at the police station."

"What do you mean he's at the police station? Like... like, he's *visiting*?"

"I mean, that's one way to put it," Phoebe says, sounding helpless. "Usually I think you'd just say he got arrested."

I nearly hit the brakes. "Arrested?! Phoebe, what the fuck?"

"Well, don't get mad at *me*! You're the one who hasn't been answering your fucking phone. They picked him up for driving drunk—and good on them for doing it. Little fucker."

Oh, god. The missed calls. I know I shouldn't while driving, but I flip desperately through my texts—the ones I didn't bother to open up until now—and they're all from Zeke, clearly hammered out of his mind and asking for a ride home from the bar. My heart sinks.

"Shit. So, what, he called *you*?"

"Yeah, after he couldn't get a hold of you or Benji—Benji had a bad breakup, story for a different day—he tried me. Will, it was awful. He was fucking *crying*."

I pinch the bridge of my nose. Even though it was Zeke who decided to get behind the wheel of a car while drunk, I still feel responsible. If I'd had my head screwed on straight, hadn't been carrying on with a woman these past couple weeks... I could've been there for him. While I was busy getting blown this evening, my brother—who I'm supposed to be looking out for—needed me. And I wasn't there.

"Fuck," I say to Phoebe. "Okay. I'm headed there now. I'll bail him out, and I'll... I'll... take care of this. Somehow."

The line clicks off, and I'm left driving in silence. I can tell Phoebe's upset with me, and I don't blame her. I'm upset with myself.

I don't know what I was thinking, letting myself lose control like that. Letting myself think my priorities belonged anywhere other than my family. I'm picturing Zeke alone in a jail cell, and yeah, even though his stupid ass deserves to be there for making such dumbfuck decisions, I also know I'm to blame. I wasn't there when he called me. I'm the one who got distracted.

I peel out of the driveway and speed off for the Hawthorne County jail. Part of me thinks I shouldn't even bail Zeke out, should just let him sit there all night and think about what the fuck he did, but I don't think I can. I've got the money—just barely—and I've already been absent enough the way it is. I can't shake the feeling that it's half my fault he's there.

It's time I get my focus straight. Letting myself get involved with Lydia hasn't been good for anyone. Carrying on with her while knowing full well I'm going to have to make good on those renovations? No matter how good the sex is—or how freeing it's been to let myself be, I don't know, the tiniest bit *vulnerable*—it's not worth the emotional distress it's going to cause.

And it's also meant I'm not there for Zeke like I should be —which is, honestly, more like my fucking old man than I care to admit. It's over with Lydia. It has to be.

At a red light, I text Ethan back. I need to do it now before I lose the nerve.

> Will: Sure thing. Permits are in, I think we can fast track the bidding.

I toss my phone onto the passenger seat, staring out at the road ahead. I don't know where this soft Will came from, but he's overstayed his welcome. I'm bailing Zeke out, taking him home, and gathering all the contacts I can to send to Ethan.

The sooner this is over and we can all move on, the better for everyone. Lydia included.

twenty-four

LYDIA

> Lydia: So, the enemy is 1000% still the enemy.

> Autumn: What happened??

> Lydia: Are you at home?

I've barely even hit send when a call from Autumn pops up on the screen. Sighing, I answer it, and she launches right in.

"Are you in the car already? Because I'm sitting here on the couch, and I can clearly see a bottle of red on the table with your name all over it."

"Ha. Is that an invitation?"

"Girl, *duh*. Patrick's in New York, you need a getaway, and I need to hear details. It's a done deal."

I hang up, grab my toothbrush, a pair of sweats, and a

comfy t-shirt to sleep in, and hop in the car. She doesn't need to tell me twice.

Autumn's lake house *is* a getaway. It's just outside of Hawthorne Bay proper, located in this gated community of gorgeous houses clustered around a picturesque little New England lake. With Autumn's husband in New York, it means we'll have the house to ourselves—the whole huge, rustic mansion on the lake. It's always so clean and cozy, with its polished hardwood floors and towering, stone fireplace. The boathouse and the dock, the gardener's cabin, the fire pit on the patio, the perfectly manicured front lawn.

I guess it's part of why she turned a blind eye to Patrick's... philandering... the way she did, although I don't think I'd ever say that to her. To each her own. It's not like I've made wonderful choices when it comes to men.

When I pull up at Autumn's house, she ushers me inside. She's got a fire going in the fireplace, and a bottle of wine under her arm, upside down wine glasses dangling between her fingers. We plop down on the sofas in front of the fire, snuggling up with the big fuzzy blankets Autumn keeps handy all over the living room.

Autumn pours me a generous glass of wine as I launch into the story. I leave out how Will and I spent this afternoon. Because honestly, I don't even want to admit it. I feel so played.

"Well, I think the fact that Will was *planning* to tell you is a good sign," Autumn points out as she downs her second glass of wine. She reaches for the bottle.

"Yeah, well, he can plan all he wants, but the fact

remains that he *didn't* tell me." I'm drinking more slowly than Autumn is, but she tops up my glass, anyway.

"I mean... that's true. He could also just be saying that because he likes sticking his penis inside you. But, like, men can get that shit anywhere. Ask me how I know." She raises an eyebrow over her wine glass.

"Yeah..."

I haven't told Autumn about the cold wave that washed through my body when I saw that text on Will's phone. I've barely even let myself register it. Because, deep down, I know that wave of despair wasn't only about the library. It was also about him. About how, apparently, the last few weeks meant nothing to him.

"I'm just saying," Autumn says, gesturing with her wine glass. She glances out the window. "It's a full moon tomorrow. Weird energy, you know? Don't give up hope yet."

I snort. I have no idea what the full moon has to do with this. "Hope of what? That Will might still talk Ethan Wilde out of that damn computer lab? Or that he'll... like..."

My voice trails off. It's the closest I've ever come to admitting to anyone that there might be more to my tryst with Will than just sex.

Autumn smirks. She knows where that sentence was going. "That he'll what?"

"Nothing. He's an asshole. All I want is for him to nix that stupid lab."

Autumn studies me. She certainly doesn't need wine to say what's on her mind, but she's even more loose lipped after a couple glasses. "I know you think preserving the library is the only way to keep a connection with your mom, but... it seems like there's got to be another way."

"What? Like sitting around reminiscing with my dad over photo albums? Get real."

I haven't spoken to my dad since he called me that morning at Brewed Awakening, wanting to introduce me to whoever it is he's "seeing." I know I should call him, but I'm still resistant to the thought of him being with anyone but my mom. There's also the fact I'm still hurt by how checked out he was for so long.

Autumn snorts. "Come on, Lydia. You know that's not what I'm saying. I just... I don't know, maybe there's a different way you can honor her memory."

I don't want to entertain the thought because I know what she's trying to get at. I eye her suspiciously. "I thought you just said there was hope for the library."

"I did, but I just want you to be prepared. You know, so you don't knee Will in the balls and get arrested for assault. And speaking of Will's balls..."

"Nope! We're not going to sit here and talk about Will Holloway's testicles."

I knock my head back and finish the wine in my glass. We're going to need to open another bottle if Autumn's going to keep talking about Will all night.

Even if it *was* just sex, there's no forgetting how safe I felt, sitting in his lap with his arms around me, the waves crashing onto the shore. The warmth of our bodies in the chill of the night air was like a microcosm of the safety we brought each other. For even those few moments, we were each other's shelter amidst the turmoil.

Jesus Christ, I need to get it together. This wine is turning me into a total sap. I grab the bottle and swig directly from it while Autumn cackles.

We spend the rest of the weekend like that, drinking wine and laughing, chatting and poking good-natured fun at one another. Autumn doesn't bring up Will again, and neither do I. Because I don't need to—no matter what I do, his face is in my head. I can even feel the memory of his low, gruff voice rumbling through my chest as he lies on top of me.

I don't even know what can be done about the library by now. Getting the board to change their design plans now feels like a distant pipe dream, and I'm realizing just how helpless I am to change any of it. But still, knowing that Will's helping the process along, that he's playing nice with Ethan Wilde and the rest of them, that they're *paying* him and he's selling out...

It's lonely as hell.

And there's not enough wine in the world to make me forget him.

twenty-five

LYDIA

I t's Sunday night when I leave Autumn's lake house and drive back to Hawthorne Bay proper. Her husband is still in New York, but I'm nervous about what I'll find out when I show up at work tomorrow morning and figure the least I can do is get a full night of sleep. If my mind can stop racing, that is.

I've heard nothing from Will since he left my house yesterday—which isn't unusual, but a part of me still hoped he'd reply to my tipsy texts. But what's left to say? I've made it very clear how much preserving the library means to me, and he's made it very clear that he's going after that project of Ethan Wilde's—meaning he's got to suck up to the guy. There for a couple weeks I'd allowed myself to hope that maybe, just maybe, he'd listen. That I'd finally be someone's first choice...

That maybe the gentle way that Will Holloway traced his rough hands across my body had less to do with lust and more to do with the connection I must have only imagined he felt. That *I* felt.

Well, joke's on me. I've said it before, and I'll say it again: I should've known better.

The lights of Hawthorne Bay have all come on as I pull off the highway and turn onto the main thoroughfare. The full moon is high in the sky, and windows glow faintly in the cool autumn night, their cozy, warm lights shining out across the harbor. The town is quiet, with everyone snug in their living rooms or sitting down at their dinner tables, gathered around fireplaces or TV screens.

Suddenly, it makes me ache for my childhood, for the kind of home life I only briefly had. I ache for my mother, for the safety of the library, the space where my mother once breathed. I know there's a glimmer of her soul left inside. I can feel it.

A ding sounds over the speakers of my car as I pull into my driveway, headlights bobbing in the darkness. I reach absently for my phone, open my email to see what the ding was about. I don't recognize the name of the sender, but it's got a ton of replies to it, so it must be some kind of mass email thread. I click on it and immediately wish I wouldn't have. Ethan Wilde's name is at the top of the first email.

What the... fuck...?

From: Ethan Wilde

To: Lydia Chandler; Undisclosed recipients

Subject: It's OFFICIAL!

Hello all,

It's with great pleasure and tons of pride that I'm able to finally announce...

The ground breaking for the Hawthorne Bay Public Library renovation project will be next Monday, October 30 at 10:00 AM!

Thanks to the diligent efforts of everyone on our board, along with the permit offices here in town, we were able to fast track the project, making it possible to break ground before winter gets going. Special thanks also go to our architect, Will Holloway, for working tirelessly this weekend to clinch those proposals.

This is a truly wonderful accomplishment that couldn't have happened without such dedicated help from so many. As chairman of the library board, I want to extend my personal thanks to everyone who had a hand in bringing this to fruition. From fundraisers and historical research to long meetings and boring email threads, this was a team effort. THANK YOU ALL!

Please don't hesitate to contact me with questions. I hope to see you all at the ground breaking.

All the best,

Ethan

By the time I'm finished reading the email, my heart's racing and my blood's gone cold, spreading all throughout my body, to my toes, my ears, my fingers. There's not a single inch of me that doesn't feel suddenly numb.

Ground breaking? How the hell? I thought we were *months* away from any actual construction. I must have read the email wrong. There's no way they could actually have pulled this off. Will didn't say anything about *this*.

But I'm not wrong.

I scan the email again, feeling sicker and sicker with each of the congratulatory replies that comes in. It's clear the others in the thread have been in the know, that I'm the one they left in the dark. Honestly, it seems I'm lucky they deemed me worthy of receiving even the announcement email.

It's over. The plans are final; the permits are issued. They're breaking ground a week from tomorrow, ripping apart any last hope I might've had—for connecting with my mother, for landmark status. For what I thought I had with Will.

Will.

Amid the despair I feel at knowing what's going to come of the project, the anger I feel at Will is rising fast and hot inside my chest.

How dare he. How fucking *dare* he.

It's not only about the renovation. It's not just about the computer lab, losing a historical landmark. It's not even only about my mother, about preserving the last shred of connection I have to her. It's about Will's betrayal—the fact that he *knew* all this, helped *facilitate* this. While I was sucking his dick in my kitchen, he was planning how to fuck me over.

I'm fucking livid. I turn the key in the ignition like I'm wrenching a screwdriver right into Will's eyeball, pull right back out of my driveway, and skid off down the street. I know where Will Holloway lives, and so help me, I will bang all night on his goddamn door until he opens it and I can see his stupid face. I want him to look me in the eye while he admits to me that he knew about the ground breaking. I want him to see my face when I tell him he's nothing to me, and never was.

Not that he'll care. I obviously meant nothing to him, either.

The light's on in Will's house as I pull up in his driveway and stalk to the front door. It's ten at night, but I ring the doorbell, anyway. I don't think he's sleeping since the light's on, but even if he is, I don't give two shits. Rise and shine, motherfucker.

The door opens. A tall, lanky guy without a shirt appears and cracks the screen door enough to stick his head out. He's got the same blond hair as Will, but his eyes are ice blue instead of Will's sapphire, and his muscles are longer, leaner. I'm pretty sure it's Will's brother, Zeke, whose shitty resume I fixed up last week. He leans against the doorframe, holding the screen door open to talk to me.

"You're the librarian," he says.

"That's me. Where's Will?"

The guy arches an eyebrow. "You seem mad. He do something?"

I blow out my breath. I don't even know this guy, and I'm losing patience. Until now, I've been riding high on adrenaline, stoking the flames of anger in my chest to make sure the reaming out I'm about to give Will is second to none.

"You could say that, yeah," I snap.

The guy in the doorway looks amused. Suddenly, I hear a

voice coming from the room beyond, and my insides seize with rage and something like fear. I push it all down. I'm not afraid of Will. Will should be afraid of *me*.

"Zeke? Who the hell's here?"

Zeke turns to smirk at his brother, then shoulder checks him as he slinks away, leaving the screen door to bang shut. He calls over his shoulder, "Good luck, bro."

Will catches the screen door with a huge hand to the glass. When he sees me standing there, I think I catch a glimpse of something soft in his eyes, but then it's gone, flickering out like a sputtering candle and replaced with something much more steely. He sets his jaw.

"Lydia, it's ten o'clock—"

"They're breaking ground on Monday and you *knew*," I snarl. "And apparently, you worked tirelessly on it all fucking *weekend*."

Will's jaw flexes, but he says nothing. He just watches me, waiting for me to get whatever I need to say out. He knows I'm not done.

"This whole time—the last three weeks—you—*I...*" I can't even get the words out right. What started as an unfurling of rage has fizzled into a dramatic mess, and I can hear my voice breaking as I grope for the words I need. "You *played* me. You fucking *played* me."

"I didn't play you."

"Yeah? Well, I'd like to hear what you call it then, because tricking a woman into thinking she might actually mean something to you, only to turn around and help pull *this* on her is quite the stunt."

Will rubs his jaw, like I've punched him in the face or

something. "You knew from the beginning what I was hired to do, Lydia. And you knew—still know—how much rides on this for me. I never kept any of that from you."

I scoff. "But you made me believe you hold sway with Ethan. You made it seem like you could change the plans."

At this, Will doesn't say anything. But I'm still fuming. I'm not letting him off that easily. I want him to feel what he's done to me, how he's messed everything up. I want him to feel what I feel.

"Really, Will," I say, my voice dripping with disdain. "Your mom's dead, too. You, of all people, should know what it's like to want to keep some part of your mother alive. But you couldn't even give me *that*—"

"Lydia." Will's voice is different now. I can't tell if it's pleading or pitying, but there's something raw beneath the gruffness. "Stop. Your mom's not coming back. It doesn't matter whether you keep every single brick of that stupid library in place or a bomb drops and turns it to charred fucking earth. Your mom is gone. *Gone*."

I step back like he's slapped me. I just stare at him, all the angry words I had lined up like munitions suddenly wiped clear out of my mind.

He softens his tone. "I'm sorry. That was... harsher than I meant it to be. But Lydia, the point still stands. Your mom's not—"

"Stop. Talking."

I barely even know I'm speaking until the words are out and Will, obviously knowing what's best for him, has already shut his damn mouth. The white-hot anger I felt just seconds ago has been replaced by a flood of aching, dizzying hurt. Not only has Will just said aloud the very thing I've been trying desperately not to believe for so many years, but he's said it in the meanest way possible, at the worst possible moment. Suddenly, it is crystal clear that Will Holloway is not who I thought he was.

And then, reaching back to that intimate moment when Will had me in his arms, I take the lowest blow I can think of.

"You're just like your dad, Will," I spit. "I should've known better than to trust that you meant a single word you said. You strung me along, made me think I might actually mean something to you—but in reality you had other plans. That's right, isn't it? You're as selfish as he was, and you fucking know it."

He stares at me. Something slackens in his mouth. I can't read what's behind his expression, but I don't bother. I'm spent, and I can feel tears pricking my eyes and a lump rising in my throat. I turn on my heel and storm down the sidewalk, knowing that if I spare so much as a glance back at Will, who's still standing in the doorway, I'll absolutely lose it.

When I get into my car and start the engine, I risk a look back at the house. But Will's no longer there. The front door is shut, solid and unmoving. He's gone back in the house. He doesn't care.

The hurt's too deep. It's over. The landmark project is over. My connection with Mom is over. And, the thing I'm scared to admit might hurt most of all, Will and I are over. I only make it half a block before the tears come and I break down into a mess of shuddering sobs.

WILL

I can't even bring myself to watch Lydia as she stalks down the sidewalk and gets in her car. I let the screen door bang shut and slam the front door so hard the living room shakes.

"Jesus Christ, Will." Zeke appears in the doorway, a beer in one hand and a bottle opener in the other. "Shut that thing a little harder, would ya?"

I don't answer, just storm past him down the hallway and to the kitchen. I snatch a beer out of the fridge and bang it on the counter to get the top off. I don't even care that I left behind a chip in the granite. Swigging down half the beer in one gulp, I slam it down on the counter and wipe my mouth with the back of my hand.

Zeke's leaning against the counter, staring at me. He hasn't even opened his beer yet. "Will... bro..."

I slog down the other half of the beer and reach for another. Zeke doesn't stop me, but he's giving me the same look I usually give him, and I hate it.

He looks alarmed. "Man, I don't know what happened out there, but... take it easy. You don't drink."

I bang the bottle on the counter again, and the cap goes flying. "Take it easy? Take it *easy*? I had to pay cash I barely have to bail you out of fucking *jail*, Zeke—less than twenty-four hours ago—and you're telling me to take it *easy*?"

Zeke raises his hands in surrender. "Okay. Yes. Will, one. Zeke, zero. But, like, I don't see what that's got to do with—"

"I'll *tell* you what it's got to do with it," I shout. "I have spent the last twenty-two years trying to be what our piece of shit dad was not. Trying to be some kind of father figure for you, for Benji. And Phoebe. Trying to be the backbone of this family. And all for fucking *nothing*."

Zeke's throat bobs as he swallows hard. "Because I drove drunk?"

"*Yes*, because you drove drunk," I snap. "And because you're sitting here on your ass in my house day in and day out, too lazy to get a job because you're out fucking ghosts at the harbor."

The corners of Zeke's mouth twitch. "That's not your fault. And—please don't bite my head off—none of that has anything to do with the librarian."

I down the second beer in a single long chug and chuck the empty bottle at the fridge, where it shatters across the floor into a million fractals.

Across the counter, Zeke flinches. "Fuck, Will. Can you just... chill out?"

I grab beer number three. Bang. Pop. Swig. The edges of my vision are swimming now, and the warmth of the alcohol as it hits my bloodstream is beginning to soften the red-hot anger I feel at myself into something darker. Something more like despair. I sink down to the kitchen floor and rest my head against the cabinets, barely even noticing the shards of broken glass beneath me.

I close my eyes, letting the start of drunkenness wash over me. "I fucking failed, Zeke."

"Failed...?"

"I'm just like Dad. I tried so fucking hard not to be, but I just... am."

Zeke starts picking his way across the kitchen floor toward me. Broken glass crackles beneath his feet. He crouches down next to me, takes the now empty third beer from my hand. "Bro, what the fuck are you even talking about?"

"Get me another beer."

"No."

I groan, banging the back of my head against the cabinet. "Don't you get it? Not only can I not even keep this fucking family on track, but I just broke Lydia's goddamn heart. And that woman, bitchy as she may be, is so pure, so—so—so *good*, and I just... ripped her to shreds, and I didn't even mean to. I was trying *not* to. Dad was right."

Zeke's quiet a moment, sipping his beer. "Did Dad say you were like him?"

I don't answer, which is clear enough.

"Dude," Zeke says. "You are *nothing* like Dad. I haven't seen him since I was, like, seven, and even I know he's a complete douchebag. You are *good*, Will. You're my brother, but you're ten times the father Dad was. Hell, probably a hundred times. And the fact that I make shit decisions some-times isn't on you."

I still don't say anything. Zeke's words are swirling into the alcoholic fog that's making a fuzzy mess of my brain. I barely ever drink, and pounding three beers in a row is proving to be a lot for my bloodstream, although it's certainly starting to numb me, which is what I wanted.

Zeke gives my shoulder a friendly pinch. "Come on, man. Let's get you to bed. You'll feel better when you can think straight."

He grips my biceps and starts to lift me up. I let him, using the cabinets for leverage as I struggle to stand, sliding on the broken glass that litters the floor.

And then I hiss. Suck in a sharp breath. From the corner of my eye, there's a flash of light that almost blinds me, but it's gone before I can turn my gaze.

"What the fuck was that?" I ask, my voice suddenly sharp.

Zeke looks alarmed. "What the fuck was what?"

I'm about to answer him, but the flash of light comes again. When I turn to look for it, it's gone, but a cold is creeping down my spine, washing through my hands and feet and ribcage, and I know exactly what it is. I've been here before. Just not for nineteen years.

"Fuuuuuck," I yell, shrugging free of Zeke's grasp.

"Holy shit, Will! You need to get a grip on yourself."

I hurl myself forward, gripping the counter, trying desperately to pull myself away from the cold that's now seeping into every inch of my body. The flickering light is back again, hanging out at the corner of my field of vision.

The more the alcohol warms my blood, the sharper the light gets, the colder my body feels.

I know exactly what's happening, but I'm powerless to stop it. The grief. The anger. The alcohol. The heartbreak. They've all converged into one, and they're too strong for my grip. The energetic wall I've spent so many years holding up with every ounce of mental strength I can find is dissolving.

And something's getting in.

I squeeze my eyes shut, frantically trying to center myself, grasping at every strand of thought, every wisp of concentration. I just need to focus. Keep the wall intact.

"Will..." Zeke's voice is shaky. "I can see her."

As soon as he says it, so can I. And I know exactly who she is, although I don't know how.

She's Lydia's mom.

The spirit hovers somewhere above the spray of broken beer bottles, both here and not here, a shadow if a shadow could be made of light. She's gorgeous, shimmering, something between a woman and a wispy, gleaming ray of moonlight. She takes my fucking breath away.

I grit my teeth, still digging my mental heels in, trying to keep that brilliant, shimmering woman from getting any closer. I know if I let go now, I may never be able to take myself completely back. The switch will be flipped, and the spirits that swirl around me will know it. I'll be fair game. I'll—

A gust of shimmering coolness wraps around me, bringing with it the unmistakable hint of vanilla. The spirit's reminding me, nudging me back to what I most want to not have to think about right now: Lydia.

I squeeze my eyes shut, breathing in that beautiful, memory-laden scent. With my eyes closed, I no longer see the silvery tendrils of Lydia's mom's spirit, but the coolness remains. And in the darkness of my mind, a flash of memory plays out.

Lydia's porcelain skin on mine. Her delicate frame in my arms as the fire next to us crackles, the waves washing up on the shore. That still-hopeful smile she wore when she told me about her mom, when she realized that she and I were not so different after all. The way her dark eyes shone when she saw that banister—and the way they bore no light at all when she showed up on my doorstep an hour ago.

And I realize suddenly what I think I've known for a while now, but which I didn't yet have the strength to believe. I would do anything for this woman. She saw right through my bullshit, and she expected better of me than I gave her. And I'll be damned if I'm going to let her down again.

Summoning every ounce of mental strength I can muster, I focus my entire self on one thing: the wall. Every cell, every fiber, every wisp and spark of energy. It's all there. I hold it in my mind's eye for one more moment, feel the rush and pulse of my blood.

And then I let it all come shattering down.

twenty-seven

WILL

I'm still gripping the counter, eyes squeezed shut. All I can hear is the heavy rasp of my breath, the pounding of the blood in my ears.

Lydia's mom is gone. The only trace of her is the shattered shards of energy—what used to be my wall—that curl around my feet like plumes of silvery smoke.

"Will," Zeke breathes. He's backed against the fridge. "What. The actual. Fuck."

I glance at him, but I don't answer. I'm suddenly hit with a wave of exhaustion so intense it feels like I might never catch my breath. The room is still echoing.

The thing is, despite how absolutely wrecked I feel, there's something electric coursing through me. The blue of Zeke's eyes is more vivid. The moonlight streaming in through the window is brighter, more defined. Even my body feels more alive, like it's been hit with a sudden pulse of starlight, and I've sobered up completely. If I listen, I can feel the whisper of spirits around me, crawling over my skin. Making themselves known.

After nineteen years, the wall is gone. And I'm unfiltered, undiluted.

My voice breaks the silence as I turn to Zeke. "Did you... see that? Or did I just feel it?"

Zeke huffs out a shaky laugh. "Oh, I saw it. That shit was crazy. What *was* that?"

"It was... that was Lydia's mom. The spirit."

"The librarian?"

"Yeah. She died when Lydia was ten. The library was Lydia's connection to her mom—that's what this whole thing is about. And now Lydia's mom showed up here, to *me*, and..."

"Okay, but what the hell was that... that..." Zeke waves a hand wildly, trying to find the right word. "That *explosion*?! You shut your eyes all tight and started breathing all heavy, and I legit thought you were dying, and then suddenly there's this silvery fucking *fireworks* show in your kitchen!"

I rub my jaw. Zeke's description of what just happened tracks. That's about how it all looked in my mind, too.

"That was my wall. Shattering."

Zeke raises his eyebrows. "Your wall? As in, your keep-the-ghosts-out wall? Holy shit..."

"Yeah."

"How'd she do it, though? Are you okay? I've never had them doing anything against my will before. Not that there's much they *could* do that'd be—"

"She didn't do it. I did. I'm the one who shattered it."

The realization hits me hard. Saying it out loud makes it

real. I'm still trying to figure out how to feel about the hum of energy I can feel around me. My mind's no longer used to the frequency, and the whispers seem to reverberate through every corner.

Zeke stares at me. It's obvious his mind is running through every possibility, turning and twisting and flipping the pieces until they fit together. His eyes narrow, and then his face breaks out into a devilish grin. "Oh, bro. You've got it *bad* for this chick."

"Yeah. I do." I hold my brother's gaze. "But this isn't done. And I need your help—so zip your trap and sit down. We're calling Benji."

Surprisingly, Zeke buttons it. He hops up onto the counter and watches as I dial Benji on FaceTime. When our middle brother answers, he's got a toothbrush hanging out his mouth and is wearing sweats and a grungy white tank top, the kind you get in three packs at Walgreens. His hair is all over the place and the dark circles that ring his eyes are downright alarming.

Shit. That breakup Phoebe mentioned must be hitting him harder than I realized.

"Benji."

Benji props the phone against something and holds up a finger, signaling for me to wait. He spits his toothpaste into the sink and gargles some water. "What's up?"

"How fast can you get here?"

Benji knits his perfect brows together. He frowns. Clearly, the thought of driving down from Boston in the middle of the night isn't something he's excited about. "Hold up. Why?"

I groan. Adrenaline is still coursing through me, and although everything makes perfect sense in my head, I know I must be skipping the important parts because Benji and Zeke are both still looking at me like I've gone nuts.

Breathe, Will. Breathe. Slow the fuck down.

"Uhhh," I start, scratching my beard. I glance at Zeke to make sure he's listening, too. They both need to hear this. "Okay. Here's the deal. Remember that librarian Zeke told you I fucked? Well, I did. I mean, I hadn't at that point. But then I did, and—whatever. It doesn't matter. The point is, I'm in love with this woman. Okay? And the library—the same one I'm supposed to be renovating—is the only connection she had left with her mom, who died when she was ten. She trusted me not to modernize the library beyond recognition, but I fucking *did*, and did it behind her back, no less, and I broke her goddamn heart. I tried so hard not to get involved with her for fear of hurting her that what did I do? Ended up hurting her anyway."

I give a harsh laugh and continue.

"So Lydia hates me. I deserve it. But her mom's been trying to get my fucking attention for weeks now, and it took me getting shitfaced for her to finally be able to come through at all. When everything started to spin... she seized her chance."

I pause again, catching my breath. Zeke's staring at me, and Benji is completely silent on the other end of the line. "My wall's gone. I let it go."

"You mean... like, completely?" Benji asks.

"Yeah, man," Zeke pipes in. "It literally *shattered*. Wicked cool, honestly."

"Well, shit," Benji says. "I never thought I'd see the day."

"You and me both."

I scrub a hand down my face. I'm trying so hard not to let the whispers that tug at the edges of the room, seeping in from who knows where, who knows when, distract me. But I need to hurry and get to the point about what we need to do. I want to do it *tonight*, and I need my brothers on board.

"So, now that I'm back in the always delightful world of psychic apparitions," I continue, letting the sarcasm creep in because, honestly, being able to feel the angsty dead people floating around you is *not* as great as the movies make it seem, "I've realized I've been an absolute fucking idiot. It may be too late for me to save the library for Lydia—but I can sure as hell keep the connection with her mom alive. I was just too selfish, too obsessed with that fucking wall and erasing every little bit of Dad, that I didn't even realize it until now."

"Aww," Zeke coos. "It's like if Casper the Friendly Ghost had a sexy ending." He bats his eyelashes at me. "Can I keep you?"

I punch him in the arm. "Laugh all you want. At least I can remember Lydia's name."

"Ooh. I'll bet she can't remember yours—"

Benji interrupts. "Zeke, shut up. Will, what do you need from us?"

"I need you to get your ass down here, stat." My voice is gruff as I point a finger at Zeke, letting him know he's included in this order as well. I look back at Benji. "And bring the spirit board. We've got a ghost to summon."

twenty-eight

WILL

Zeke: Duuuuude. Benji. Where the hell are you?

Benji: Driving.

Zeke: Well, put the pedal to the metal! We've got to get this seance going.

Phoebe: Zeke, this is the group chat. Also, you guys are doing a seance without me?!

Will: You're invited to the next one.

Phoebe: Wait. WILL is joining this seance?!

Will: Long story. Fill you in later.

"Did you seriously forget the matches?"

"I was in a rush, man!"

Benji glares at me in the dark, and I shrug. Just five minutes ago, he pulled up in my driveway, having sped all the way from Boston.

Now we're at the library, trying to get this party started. We drove here together, figuring it'd be less conspicuous if we park a couple blocks away and keep a low profile. Something tells me it wouldn't go over too well if the project architect was caught trespassing in the middle of the night with candles and a Ouija board.

Since Lydia's mom appeared to me in my kitchen, Benji wondered if we could hold the seance there, but I know we can't. It won't work otherwise. It has to be in the library, although I'm not sure why. I can just feel it. I can't help but think that if I hadn't been so drunk, maybe Lydia's mom would've been able to get her message through, and we wouldn't even have to be *doing* this.

But then again, I think it was the getting drunk that allowed her to come through at all. So here we are. I never thought I'd be sitting down to intentionally summon a spirit ever again in my life, but I'll do what I have to do. For Lydia.

"Oh, you two goody goodies," Zeke mutters as he butts in between us. He pulls a lighter out of his pocket and lights the tall, black candles that Benji has arranged in the middle of the foyer floor. "You think I'm walking around without a light? You're welcome."

The whites of Benji's eyes roll in the darkness, but he ignores Zeke. Instead, he unfolds the spirit board and places the planchette in the very center.

We're crouched around the makeshift seance we've set up in the library foyer. Although we're alone inside the building, we keep our voices low. I'm already afraid the candles are going to attract the attention of anyone driving by, but Benji insists we can't do it without them.

"Give me your hands." Benji sits cross-legged and reaches his hands out, palms up, for me and Zeke. "I'll do the grounding, but we've got to establish a connection."

Zeke takes Benji's hand and grins. "You don't even wanna know where my hand's been."

"Zeke," I growl. "Focus."

It's been six years since I last tried to initiate contact with a spirit. My mom. That time it was all four of us—Benji, Zeke, Phoebe, and me. I told myself that if Mom would only show up, would let me feel her presence for just the glimmer of a moment, I'd let down my wall. But she never showed up, never answered. Benji said it was good she didn't, that it meant she had no unfinished business. That she was at peace.

I close my eyes. I hope bringing Lydia and her mom some peace will bring me a little of my own.

"Okay," Benji says, his voice cutting through the stillness. "We are reaching out to the spirit of—oh, shit. What's her name, Will?"

"Fuck. I don't know. Lydia's mom."

"We're reaching out to the spirit of Lydia's mom. Lydia's mom, please join our circle when you are ready."

We sit in silence for a moment, the only sound the flickering of the candle flames and the occasional creak of the building. There's still the dull hum of spirits in the back of my mind, and I'm having a hard time concentrating. I really hope this shit gets less annoying the more used to it I get. It must, because I never hear any of my siblings complain.

Benji tries again. "Lydia's mom. If you're here... if you're here, Will needs to talk to you."

As soon as he says my name, a freezing wind whips through the room and my eyes fly open. It's like the spirit was just waiting, wanting to make sure of what we were really there for. I can't see her yet, but I can sure as hell feel her. And even though my body's gone cold as ice, I can tell the spirit's warm. I can tell she's every bit as gentle as her daughter.

"She's here," Zeke says, his eyes wide. He looks a little awestruck. And no wonder—the presence in the room with us is magnificent.

But I'm not surprised. Lydia's mom must've been one hell of a kick-ass woman to raise such a resilient, determined daughter.

Benji closes his eyes again. The three of us are still holding hands, the spirit board and candles in the middle of our little circle. It's been so long since I've summoned a spirit, I'm completely out of my element. So I try to sit taller, emulating what Benji's doing.

"Lydia's mom... will you tell me your name? It's weird to keep calling you Lydia's mom when I don't even know Lydia."

I'm struck by how casual Benji is. It's not what I was expecting at all. I don't know if I thought some kind of Haunted Mansion head in a crystal ball was going to come floating down while speaking Latin or what, but I'm kind of relieved it's just Benji in his flannel button down, sitting barefoot on the library floor, kicking it with Lydia's mom.

Suddenly, the planchette in the middle of the spirit board starts whipping between letters. Zeke and I lurch forward to watch, announcing the letters aloud as the planchette moves.

"S... O..."

"Sophia."

Zeke's head jerks around to glare at Benji. "Show off! Why do we even bother bringing the board if you're just gonna beat us to it?"

Benji shrugs. "Sorry. It's so you guys can ask questions, too. You might get the yes/no answers faster than me."

It's kind of annoying that Benji's the only one of us who actually got the ability to communicate with the spirits the other three of us can only see—or feel?—but it's why I need him here. We've never had a clue why it ended up that way, with Benji being the one who can talk to them, but it's always irritated Zeke. I guess he must not like it when he can't hear the dirty talk from the ghost chicks he's fucking.

"Sophia," Benji says again. "Thanks, Sophia. You've been trying to get Will's attention, right? Can you tell us why? What is it you need to say?"

"Yes or no questions, my ass," Zeke mutters.

Benji ignores him, cocking his head to the side in concentration. His eyes are glazed over, his gaze distant. His posture is completely erect, and he's sitting so still he's like some kind of wax figure. He's about as perfect looking as one, too. He and Phoebe look like Mom, all cinnamon brown eyes and thick, chestnut hair—something *I* have always been a little jealous of.

"She's saying... something about paper? Maybe she wants us to get out paper so she can write something? No, that's not it."

Benji's speaking aloud, passing along the information as it comes to him. I've never been sure exactly *how* Benji communicates with spirits, whether he hears words in his head or sees visions across his mind or just has some kind of feeling. He told me once it was like watching a montage of video footage that's overlaid with the occasional flash of words. I still don't get it, but however he does it, he does it well.

"Oh, wait. She's flipping a bunch of pages. It's a book! It's something about a book. Will, she's trying to tell you something about a book that belongs to Lydia."

I frown, but I feel the hair on my arms bristle. "A book? What, like a library book?" The planchette flies to the *no* space on the board. "Okay, then. Not a library book."

"Lydia's writing a book?" Zeke suggests.

The planchette gives a hop and thunks back down. *No.*

"Hang on," Benji says. "It's here in the library. There's a box..."

"I saw that office," Zeke groans. "That place is a *mess* of boxes. Come on. Get your shit together, Sophia. You've gotta give us something other than *that.*"

"Excuse me?" I bark. Benji hisses at me to be quiet, and I lower my voice. "That's Lydia's goddamn mom you're talking to, fuckwad."

"Yeah, and she's gonna bitch slap both of you—or I will

—if you guys don't shut it." Benji gives our hands a squeeze that I'm honestly surprised doesn't break my damn bones.

But it works. We shut up.

Suddenly, the chill in the room turns to ice. A silvery mist materializes in the air, wrapping itself around me like a freezing blanket. It's comforting in its weight, but goose-bumps break out all over my skin.

The mist swirls, glistening like moonlight, as it—she—shifts fluidly, seamlessly from vapor to woman, woman to vapor, and back again. Unlike the ghosts I remember from my younger years, Sophia Chandler isn't just a human form. She's somehow lighter, more radiant.

"Her soul's free," Benji murmurs, as though reading my mind. "She's here by choice."

My brothers and I are silent for a moment, mesmerized by the beauty of Lydia's mom, by the stillness that's fallen on the room. But then—I sense a shift in energy.

An urgency.

"Get up, Will," Benji says. He releases my hand. "She wants to show you something, not tell you. I think there's an actual book here she wants you to find."

"Me? Why can't she—"

But the misty, swirling light is lifting me up, raising me to my feet. Nudging me toward the office. I can actually feel the pressure of an icy hand on my back, its dainty fingers pressing into my jacket in a way that feels completely real. Because it *is* real. And it blows my fucking mind.

"She's, like... pushing me," I call over my shoulder to Benji and Zeke as I stumble toward the office. I barely even need to walk, so determined is Sophia to get me where she wants me to go.

"Just let her," Benji says. "I'm still on her wavelength. This is what she wants."

The knob of the office door turns on its own—or rather, the gorgeous, shimmering mist that is Sophia Chandler turns it—and I'm shoved inside. Not slowing down for a second, Lydia's mom continues to push me, icy hand on my back, toward a stack of boxes in the very corner of the room, next to Nancy's desk. It's dark in the office, but in the silvery half light Sophia casts around the room, I think I can make out the scrawled handwriting on the side of the box: *Special editions*.

Before I even know what's happening, the box on the top of the stack topples down, spilling books all over the floor.

"Jesus," I mutter under my breath. I hope Lydia's mom didn't see me flinch.

Another box crashes to the floor. And another.

"What the fuck are you doing in there, Will?!"

I can tell by Zeke's voice that the loud crashes and thuds have him worried, but he's trying to play it off like it's funny. I hear Benji tell him to shut up, so I don't answer. I need to focus on what Lydia's mom is trying to show me.

I'm standing in a sea of half open books and bent covers. I'm pretty sure if Lydia saw this mess of books she'd have a heart attack, especially if these things are really special editions. But I'm not about to second-guess the ghost of Sophia Chandler. She clearly knows what she's after, and hey —she *was* the librarian here.

The box opens, and books go flying. They're hitting the

walls, covers flapping, thudding to the floor. It's a whole fucking storm of books, and I *really* hope I won't have to clean all this up, but—

It stops. The crashing goes silent. Sophia urges me forward toward the box, and I lift the flaps, reaching inside it. On the bottom lies a single book. I lift it out, feeling the smoothness of the worn cover in my palms.

It's a Nancy Drew book. *The Secret in the Old Attic.*

"Okay…" I say aloud. I'm not even sure Lydia's mom can hear me, or if I'll be able to hear her if she answers.

The book cracks open in my hand. A silvery breeze ripples through the pages as they flutter to the title page, where a small, flat envelope has been pressed between the pages. When I turn the envelope over in my shaking hands, I can see that Lydia's name has been written across the front in beautiful, flowing script.

"Is this… for Lydia?" I ask.

"Planchette says yes," Zeke calls from beyond the door.

"And the book…?"

The envelope slides back into place and the book slams shut.

"The book's for her, too?"

"That's a yes," comes Zeke's voice again.

Wasting no time, the spirit of Lydia's mom shoves me back out into the foyer and the office door clicks shut. But she doesn't push me back into the circle with Benji and Zeke. She keeps her firm, yet still gentle hand between my shoulder blades and guides me toward the front door.

"Guys, she's not letting up," I hiss over my shoulder.

Benji grins at me from behind the still flickering candles.

He flicks a hand at me. "Don't worry about us. You do what you need to do."

Sophia leads me out of the library and into the chill, night air. As she nudges me down the sidewalk and toward my truck, the hazy glow of the full moon streams down to light our way. Between the cold of the night and the icy mist of the spirit hovering around me, it's absolutely freezing. But my heart is racing, the blood is pumping through my veins, and I feel more alive than I have in a long, fucking time. And when Lydia's mom opens the door of my pickup and practically shoves me up into the cab, I look down at the book that I'm still holding in my hands.

This time, I don't need Benji to tell me what I'm supposed to do. I know. Beyond the shadow of a doubt, I know exactly what Lydia Chandler needs from me.

And goddamnit, I'm going to come through.

 twenty-nine

LYDIA

I wake up to the sound of pounding on my door. At first, I think I must be dreaming it, like I'm caught somewhere between sleeping and waking, and my mind is going haywire. So I roll over, bury my face into the pillow.

But then it comes again. *Bam. Bam bam bam.*

This time, I jerk awake. Pushing myself up on my elbows, I stare groggily at the clock on the nightstand, willing the numbers to make sense. It's two thirty in the morning. I'm not sure what woke me, but I lay awake, mind racing and tears soaking my pillow, until almost two—so I know it had to have been *something*. I listen again. Someone's pounding on the door.

Fear seizes my gut. Frantically, I swipe through my phone and pull up the Ring doorbell app. No way am I, a single woman home alone, going out there to answer that damn door without knowing who's out there.

When the camera comes on the screen, my heart speeds up. Because there, right on my front step, is Will Holloway, looking raw and undone and as ruggedly sexy as ever. Pounding on my door. There's something electric about him I can't quite place—something in the way he carries himself, the broad span of his muscular shoulders. Or maybe it's his deep blue eyes that somehow manage to sparkle despite the fuzzy camera graphics. I don't know.

I run to the kitchen and grab a rolling pin. I don't know what he's here for. The tender man I thought I knew would never hurt me, but now... I'm not sure I ever knew Will as well as I thought I did. And it never hurts to play it safe. Still gripping my rolling pin, I stand on the inside of the door, trying to find my voice. I'm not stupid enough to just open the door when a man pounds.

"What do you need?"

The pounding stops, and I hear Will's voice from the other side of the door. "Oh, thank god. I thought you'd never wake up. Lydia, I've got to talk to you. Please open the door."

A harsh laugh escapes my chest. "Why should I? So you can break my heart a little more?"

"No. So I can look you in the eye and tell you what a

complete fucking asshole I've been. That I'm crazy about you. That I've *been* crazy about you from the minute you spilled that damn coffee all over me and stole my heart."

I unlock the door. Open it. And there is Will, staring out at me from the most broken, sapphire eyes I've ever seen in my life. He doesn't say anything, doesn't move. Just takes me in, his gaze clinging to mine in the most disarming way possible. The electricity that radiates off him is absolutely intoxicating.

The corner of his perfect mouth turns up slightly. "Hey, beautiful."

"Hey."

I have no idea what to say. With the way he's looking at me, I can barely think.

"I'm sorry." Will rakes a callused hand through his hair. "You have no idea how *fucking* sorry I am. And I know there's nothing I can say that will fix it. I fucked up. You gave me your trust, and I broke it—and I get it if you want me to get the fuck out, so you never have to see me again. I don't expect you to forgive me."

Will pauses. The moonlight filters down through the brittle, bare branches of the trees, casting a silvery glow around us. The neighborhood is quiet. There's no world in which his wild pounding didn't wake anyone else up, but so far, no one's stirring. It's just me and him.

Will continues, and I swear I hear his voice crack. "But Lydia, I have to tell you something—even if you don't forgive me—because you need to know. It's important to me that you know."

I swallow. No one's ever looked at me the way Will is looking at me right now. "Know what?"

"That I will do whatever it takes. Be whatever you need. Give up whatever I have to. Because you're worth so much more than you give yourself credit for. You're worth everything."

He takes a step forward, closing the space between us. He looks down at me, runs a gentle thumb along my jawline. His chest is so close, so warm even in the bite of the autumn night air, I can feel his heart beating.

"Lydia." His voice is soft, rich. And his eyes. Fuck. They're like ocean waves, and he's gazing at me so tenderly I can hardly breathe.

"Yeah?" My lips move, but I'm honestly not even sure if I'm making sound.

Will tucks a strand of my hair behind my ear. His fingers tangle in my loose hair, cupping the back of my head gently. "I'm done trying to fight it. I'm crazy, off-my-rocker, seeing-things madly in love with you."

His lips skim my forehead, and he pulls back to look at me. He's got this small, almost nervous smile going, but he doesn't wait for me to speak. He presses the pad of his finger to my lips. "I had some help tonight. From someone who knows you really well. I'm going to give you two some time, okay? If you want to see me at some point, even years down the road, I'll be here. And if not..." He runs a hand through his hair. "If not, that's alright. I'll respect it. Just love yourself for me, okay?"

All I can do is stare at him. My body's all tingly, my heart's racing, and I'm met with the overwhelming urge to chuck the rolling pin away and wrap my arms around his solid waist. Pull him close and bury my face in his chest. Breathe in his spicy, pine scent.

But Will just presses something into my hands, kisses the top of my head, and turns and walks back down the sidewalk. I watch him get into his pickup and pull away before I look down at what he just gave me. It's a worn, faded copy of the twenty-first Nancy Drew book: *The Secret in the Old Attic*. I'd know it anywhere—it's just like the one my mom and I used to read together all those years ago. I suck in my breath. Is this...?

It has the same frayed corners, the same half page ripped out in the back. The *M* on the title is almost completely rubbed off, just like in the copy we used to read. Holy shit. How did Will know my mom and I used to read this book? And how the hell did he get his hands on it? And who the fuck was he talking—

My thoughts stop mid-sentence. Where just a moment ago Will stood on the sidewalk, I swear I see a shimmering streak of silver light. I blink a couple times. Maybe I'm seeing things. But the shimmering mist is still there, and it's dancing, rippling, swirling toward the book. Will said he had help tonight. I'd thought he meant the book had helped him somehow, but now I've got a strange feeling that he meant something else entirely.

He said some*one* who knows me. He said you *two* should have some space.

And then I realize, with a jolt of joy and wonder and utter disbelief, that there's a reason this silvery mist seems so excited for me to open this book.

"Mom?" I whisper. I must be going batshit crazy.

But the book flips open, almost on its own, and I know she must have done it. I watch as she flips through the pages until she finds what she's looking for. An envelope with my name on it.

With shaking hands, I tuck the book under my arm and open the envelope. There's a letter inside, which I can already see is laced with Mom's delicate, loopy handwriting. A wave of longing hits me. It's been so long since I've seen that handwriting. I can almost see her slim hand, imagine it moving across the page. Unless this mist can somehow hold a pen, my mom must have written this for me years ago.

I unfold the paper and begin reading.

> Dear Lydia,
> If you're reading this, it means you've had to say goodbye to me.

Straight out the gate, the tears come. I wipe them away and continue on.

> It also means that there are tons of things we didn't get to do together. Experiences we didn't get to share. Conversations we never got to have. This letter will never make up for the time we don't have, but I hope it'll be comforting. I hope you can read it and feel me nearby.
> I won't get the chance to show you how to be

a woman—and being a woman can be tough. But you can do it. You are my strong, strong girl. I don't know how your dad's going to do without me, but there's one thing I'm sure of, and it's that you are going to come through this an even stronger, even more loving person. Take care of your dad for me. He needs you, even if he doesn't show it.

Which reminds me... When it comes to taking care of people, please take care of yourself, but don't become so strong you don't let anyone else take care of you. When the time comes—many years from now—make sure you find a man (or woman?!) who loves you deeply. Who puts you first. And don't settle for anything less. You are worthy of being someone's #1 priority, and I need you to promise me you'll remember that. Okay?

And Lydia? I may not be with you in person, but I promise you: I won't be very far away. In fact, I suspect that if you only just talk to me out loud, I'll be able to hear it. I thought you might want a tangible reminder of me, so I'm putting this note inside our special copy of Nancy Drew. Any time you feel alone, *just crack it open, read a few pages, and remember how much I love you.*

    All my love,

    Mom

I stare at the note a moment, swiping desperately at the tears to keep them from soaking through the paper. My hands are shaking, but I feel strangely light. Like there's been a boulder in my stomach these past twenty-five years, and now it's suddenly lifted.

It's all so crazy, but… it's real.

Mom. This handwritten note she never got to give me before she died. Our copy of our favorite Nancy Drew book. The swirling mist that still hovers on my doorstep. Mom's not at the library. She's here with me.

I reach out a timid hand toward the mist. It wraps around me, entwining with my fingers. This form of my mom is physically colder than she used to be, but every bit as warm inside. A sense of peace washes through me, and we stay like that for a moment longer, relishing in this strange, wonderful experience of each other.

"What do I do?" I ask. It feels weird, but I know she hears me.

The mist unwraps itself from my hand. It gathers itself up, and it's almost like Mom is looking me straight in the face. Then the silvery plume curls backward, whirling, spiraling down the steps. She makes a beeline across the sidewalk, and comes to a hovering stop in the driveway, right where Will's truck was just parked.

Mom waits a minute, making sure I'm picking up what she's laying down. I shake my head at her, chuckling. And, I swear to god, the mist *crackles*, looking like one of those fountains kids light off in the street on the Fourth of July. I'm pretty sure Mom's laughing at me.

Then, with a little twist, the plume of silvery mist begins to rise. Up, up, up... I watch her twirl, getting farther and farther away, like sparks floating up from a bonfire.

And then she's gone. The last shimmer of silvery light has faded.

I set the Nancy Drew book on the kitchen counter and pull on a pair of Keds. Mom may not have used words just now, but she got the message across. I know what I need to do. Not even bothering to grab a jacket or lock the door, I take off down the street like a bat out of hell.

<h1 style="text-align:center">thirty</h1>

WILL

Benji: How'd it go?

Zeke: Shh. Benji. Don't bother him. He's probably getting some 

Phoebe: I'm sorry…what???

Zeke:

Phoebe: What the fuck kind of seance did you guys have?!

Benji: Go back to sleep, Pheebs.

Since leaving Lydia's house, I've been driving around town trying to get my head screwed back on straight. The windows are down, and the cool night air whips through the cab of my truck as I rumble along past the harbor. I'm taking deep breaths, hoping it'll somehow calm my nerves.

Telling Lydia straight up how I feel about her was the scariest fucking thing I think I've ever done. And I still have no clue how she felt about it. But I'm trying to remind myself that that's not the important thing right now. The important thing is that I *told* her—and that I could help reunite her with her mom, even if just for a few minutes. Getting that book into the hands of her daughter was Sophia Chandler's unfinished business, and now that it's done... it won't be long before Sophia's gone for good, floating peacefully into the Great Beyond.

But Lydia's strong. She'll be okay. I'll make sure of it—if she'll let me.

My mind is a whirlwind of thoughts, and I seriously doubt I'll be getting any sleep tonight. Benji texted to say that he and Zeke were back at my place and heading to bed in the guest room, so at least there's that. Now it's just me alone with my thoughts and the electrifying whispers that call out to me from some parallel plane.

I'm so lost in my thoughts, with gazing out at the silhouetted trees as they fly past, that it takes me a minute before I glimpse the flash of movement in the rearview mirror. At first I think it's headlights, like maybe someone's come up behind me, but I haven't seen a single other vehicle on the road since I left Lydia's house. But then whatever it was I saw is gone. It must be the ghosts. I'm not used to seeing them anymore, having little glimpses of them flitting in and out of my vision. Still, I slow down to a crawl, my eyes flicking back to the mirror now and then to see if whatever it was comes back.

And then I see her in the side mirror. It's Lydia, literally sprinting along behind my truck. She's in her fucking nightgown and pumping her arms like a high school track star, hair flying out behind her. The look on her face is one of pure determination, and I honestly can't tell if she's on her way to kiss me silly or punch my fucking lights out.

I hit the brake and slow the truck to a stop, putting it in park. Lydia's absolutely booking it, and it only takes her about twenty seconds to reach my truck. As she skids to a stop and flings my door open, my heart's pounding in my chest. I still can't read the look on her face, but if this is going to be the end of us, we may as well get it over with. No use dragging things out. No use making the pain last longer than it needs to.

My entire six and a half foot frame is a ball of nerves as Lydia climbs up onto the footrest, bringing her face in line with mine. She looks at me for a minute, all breathless and disheveled and panting. She's got this coy little smile on as she brings her hands to either side of my face and says, "Will Holloway, you drive *so* fucking slow."

And then she kisses me, and it's deep and rich and electric. Her mouth moves against mine like there's no way we can ever be close enough. Like she wants to crawl inside my skin and stay there. Like she's been stranded in a desert and I'm some kind of oasis.

She's still kissing me as she hoists herself up into the cab and swings a leg over my lap, so she's straddling me. We're literally parked in the middle of the road, but neither of us so much as thinks to glance around and make sure no other cars are coming. One of us, I'm not even sure who, slams the door shut. Lydia pulls back a minute, gazing down at me with puffy, parted lips. I know she can feel me getting hard beneath her ass, especially with her nightgown all hiked up around her waist and only the thin fabric of her underwear separating her from me, but I stay perfectly still. I'm hoping we can have just one more minute like this—looking at each other with nothing else existing in the world.

I clear my throat softly, breaking the silence. "Did you…?"

I want to ask about her mom, but I also don't want to pry. My part there is done, and the rest of it is between Lydia and Sophia.

Lydia nods. "We can talk about it later. But right now…"

She trails off, and she brings her hands back to my face, stroking my jaw with the backs of her knuckles. I shiver. Her touch is absolutely delicious.

"Lydia," I start in a low voice. I hold her gaze. "I don't know how much longer I can sit with your ass pressed up against my cock like this and still keep my hands to myself."

She laughs softly. "Who says you have to?"

She grabs one of my hands and slides it under the hem of her nightgown, and that's my green light. I trail my fingers up her stomach and palm her breast, letting out a groan as my cock thickens even more in my jeans. Gently, I pull the hem of Lydia's nightgown upwards, and she gets my signal, stripping it off and tossing it onto the passenger seat, baring her breasts to me completely. The moonlight's streaming down onto the hood of my truck and the delicate curves of Lydia's figure are silhouetted against it. She's so damn beautiful.

With shaking hands, I cup one of her breasts in each hand. They're gorgeous, all pillowy and soft, and all I want to do is bury my face in them.

"Fuck," I rasp, tracing a rough finger around one of her nipples. "You're already so turned on. These things are practically begging me to suck them."

I lean forward, taking her nipple into my mouth and rolling my tongue around it. Taking as much of her breast into my mouth as I can, I suck hard and Lydia moans. My cock's straining at my jeans, like it knows that Lydia's pussy is right fucking *there*. There's no way she doesn't feel it, rock hard between her legs, because she starts grinding her hips against me. I press back, reaching around to grip her ass, and pretty soon we're rocking rhythmically together, her tit still stuffed in my mouth.

"Will." Lydia's voice is breathless in my ear. "We're in the middle of the road. Do you think any cars will come?"

I release her nipple from between my teeth and trail kisses up her chest, swipe my tongue along her collarbone. I want every single inch of this woman. Want to make every single part of her mine.

"I don't give a fuck if they do," I rasp into her ear. I feel her shiver below me. "In fact, that might be hot. They'll get a little lesson, watching how hard I'm going to make you come." Her eyes widen, and I grip her jaw in one hand, brush a kiss to her willing lips. "Because you *will* come for me, Lydia. There's nothing between us now, and there's no way I'm letting your pretty little pussy out of this truck until it's spasming around my cock. Got it?"

She just nods at me, eyes wide, and I hold her gaze as my hands find my zipper.

"Besides," I say, unzipping myself and raising my hips, Lydia still perched on my lap, to slide my jeans down."It's a full moon tonight. What's a few moans and howls?"

My bare ass is on the seat of my truck, but I don't fucking care. I'm about to bury my cock inside the gorgeous woman sitting on my lap, and the damn upholstery could not be further from my mind. I pull my fly out of the way, and my cock springs up between Lydia's legs. Lydia groans as I swipe a finger down the thin strip of fabric that's still covering her pussy. It's fucking soaked.

"That wet for me, huh," I remark, feigning surprise as I shuck my shirt off. "That's good. That'll come in handy when I impale you on my dick in a second. But beautiful, can you reach the glove box? I think there's a—"

"No."

I quirk an eyebrow at her. "I was going to say condom."

"I know. I don't want the condom. You said there's nothing between us now, so that's what I want when you're inside me, too. I want to feel every single inch of you."

Her lips are set in such a determined line that it almost makes me smile. But I hold her gaze for another moment, wanting her to be certain. "You sure?"

"Abso-fucking-lutely."

I grin at her. "Okay then."

With a growl, I push her back against the steering wheel and hook my finger inside the strip of panty that goes between her legs, pulling it to the side. Her sweet wetness is already dripping onto my fingers, and I slide a little of it around her opening before bringing my fingers to my mouth to suck them. Fisting my cock, I rub the tip against her entrance, feeling the warm slide of her wetness as I groan. I want her to feel how much I want her.

"Will," Lydia pants. "I need you in me."

I need me in her, too.

Wrapping my hands around her delicate waist, I lift her hips, lining her entrance up over the head of my cock. And then I sink into her, pulling her back down onto my lap, feeling the hug of her pussy around my length as she wraps her arms around me. She leans forward, shifting her weight onto her knees so she can ride me. I'm struck by just how close we are. No clothes. No inhibitions. No fucking latex. There's just me, her, and the sound of our heavy breathing in the pickup cab, her heart next to mine.

"You ride me so good, Lydia." I bite back a groan as she slides herself up and down on my shaft. "You *love* me so good. I don't know what I did to deserve you, but *fuck*. If you keep that up…"

I bite my lip, resisting the urge to take her by the waist again and slam myself into her. But she hasn't come yet, and I'm pretty sure I just told her we're not leaving this truck until she does. I've gotta ease up.

Grabbing her ass cheeks, I slow the rise and fall of her hips, leaning in to kiss her deeply. Then, my mouth still on hers, I say, "You came on my fingers, beautiful. You even came in my mouth. But now I want to see you come on my dick with nothing in between us."

I open the door of the cab and, my hands under her ass and my dick still sheathed inside her, I walk my feet so they're hanging out of the cab and shift my lap so Lydia's bare back is to the open door.

Lydia tenses. The night air must be cold on her skin because she's suddenly covered in goosebumps. "Will, what the fuck—"

"You trust me, right?"

Lydia's eyes search mine, but she nods.

"Then go with it. I'm going to make you feel like no one ever fucking has, and I can't do it all cramped like this. I need space to ravage you properly."

I hear what I think is a laugh as I step down from the cab, one arm holding Lydia tight against my body, and carry her around to the back of the pickup. Then, sliding my glistening cock out of her, I throw her over one shoulder and flip the hatch down.

"Holy shit, Will," Lydia giggles. From where she hangs over my shoulder, she reaches down to slap my bare ass. "This is insane. Your jeans are around your thighs. If you trip and drop me, I swear to god—"

"I'm not gonna drop you," I growl.

With one hand, I shake out the flannel blanket I keep folded in the back and smooth it out over the hatch. Gently, I set Lydia's ass down on the back of the truck. I suck in a breath. She's fully naked, and her legs are slightly spread, putting her pussy on full display in front of my face. Her cunt looks pink and wet and delicious, but there'll be plenty of hours for me to spend with my head between Lydia's legs. Right now, I need to feel our bodies entwined. And I think she needs it too, because she tugs at my arm to pull me up onto the hatch with her.

She lies back onto the blanket, and I hover over her, my knees on either side of her hips. And when her fingers clasp around my ass cheeks, pulling me into her once again, I groan with relief. Every second I have to spend outside of Lydia's body tonight is torture. I need her close to me, need to know that she feels loved. Protected. Cherished.

Lydia runs her hands along my back, traces my shoulder blades, as I thrust in and out of her. The night is cool, but our bodies and blood are hot, pulsing, the moon our own private spotlight. I bring my mouth to Lydia's again, kissing her hungrily and loving the way she writhes under me.

But now I mean business.

"Legs up, beautiful." I pause my thrusting long enough to roll Lydia's hips up, bringing her feet toward her head. "I want to be as deep in you as humanly possible while I work your clit."

Lydia does as she's told, throwing her legs over my shoulders so that every time I thrust I'm shoving in all the way to the hilt. And all the while, I'm stroking her clit, tracing little circles around it like I know she likes. Lydia's bucking her hips against me, and more than once I feel her shudder. She feels so good I can feel my own orgasm building, but I've got to hang on. Got to make sure she gets there. So I keep on. In. Circle. Out. Circle.

Her breaths are getting faster. The muscles in her pelvis tense. "Will, I'm going to—"

And then she shatters.

I press my thumb against her clit, shove my dick in as deep as it'll go, and let myself explode into her with a roar. As I come, I'm feeling *her* come. Feeling the way the walls of her pussy squeeze my cock as they spasm with pleasure. The way her nails dig into my back as she moans into my ear and I fill her up.

We stay like that for a moment, each feeling the other breathe. I keep thinking of the way Lydia glared at me that day in Brewed Awakening, like it was my fault she'd just spilled her coffee all over me. I'm also remembering how she shot daggers at me with her look alone that first day in Nancy's office. And it makes me chuckle, thinking about how we got from that to *this*.

Her in my arms. My cum inside her. As close as two people can be. And somehow, I know that after tonight our souls are even closer. All kinds of veils are being pulled back tonight.

"I love you."

Lydia's gazing up at me from the bed of the truck, and when she speaks I gather my thoughts back in and study her face. I can see the full moon reflected in her big, dark eyes. It's the first time she's told me that, and I want to remember every detail about this moment.

I brush the hair out of her eyes and kiss her forehead. "I love you too, beautiful."

Then, sliding myself out from between her legs, I flop over onto my back and lie next to her, guiding her head onto my chest.

We lie like that for a long time, me stroking her hair and her tracing delicate fingertips across my stomach. It's only when the very first streaks of purple begin to lighten the eastern sky that we pull on our clothes and hop back in the truck, holding hands across the console as we take off for home.

We spend the last two precious hours before our six thirty alarm goes off nestled together in Lydia's bed. As I snuggle into her, wrapping my arms around her tiny frame, I drift off to sleep, realizing that I don't think I'll ever let this woman sleep alone again.

LYDIA

Will: Looking good over there behind that desk, beautiful.

Lydia: Aren't you supposed to be working?

Will: I am working. It's a full time job trying to keep my eyes off you.

Lydia: Good god. We've got a long several months ahead of us.

Will: Not the only thing that's long.

Lydia: Gross.

Will: Not what you said last night.

Will: Okay. Sorry. I'll be good. Wanna go get coffee?

"You better watch where you're going with that this time."

Will nudges me playfully in the ribs as he juts his chin at my to-go cup. I roll my eyes at him and tear open a packet of sugar. "Trust me. It's not in my best interest to burn your junk, Will."

He whistles. When he gives my ass a squeeze, my head whips fiercely around to make sure no one saw it.

"Do *not*," I hiss, flicking a hand at him, barely smothering my laughter. I may be a prude, but he knows I'm enjoying his attention. In fact, I've been basking in it the whole freaking week.

We've been at the library since early this morning, getting everything ready for the ground breaking. Since the construction of the new computer lab is first on the agenda, the main part of the library will remain open, but over the past week we've had to shift things around to keep visitors away from the work zone. I'm not looking forward to having the noise of construction constantly in the background while I'm working, but at least I'm making peace with the project.

I'd be lying if I said I didn't draw a deep, shaky breath when we got here and I saw the tarps the construction team put up. It really hit me... The building I loved so much, that provided so many sacred hours for me when I needed it most, will never be the same. It's the end of an era, and endings are always hard.

But now I know. I don't need a building to stay connected to Mom. This morning I hopped down from Will's pickup and strode toward the library, clutching my Nancy Drew book under my arm and knowing my mom's still with me, building or no building. I've got our book, I've got her letter, and I've got the happiness that comes from knowing she's been looking out for me all this time. And still is.

My encounter with Mom even gave me the courage to call my dad. We've still got years' worth of stuff to work through together, and that's going to take time and effort. But I told him I want to meet Shelley, and he told me he's been sober for one hundred days now. It's not a happy ending for Dad and me yet, but it's a start. A baby step in the right direction.

I know Mom will be happy, and that makes me happy.

As Will followed me up the library sidewalk this morning, I could tell he was nervous. Like he was holding his breath or something, waiting to see if this past week we spent together would still hold this morning. Or if I'd break down, or turn around and pound his chest with my fists. I could tell when he came to stand by me on the front stairs, wrapping an arm around my shoulders, that he still blames himself. And even though it may take time, I'll do whatever I can to help dispel that guilt.

Because Will gave me more than a building. He gave me Mom—for one last time.

I don't think I would've believed him if he'd told me before I saw her. That he has this... *gift*. There hasn't been time for him to tell me all the details, but he told me the gist of it. How the gift comes from his dad's side and all his siblings have it. How he put up some kind of energetic wall over a decade ago to keep the spirits out of his life, trying to distance himself from anything that might make him turn out like his dad.

And then how, through what he described as the perfect storm of moon phase, alcohol, and despair, my mom managed to reach through that wall and snag his attention.

I know there was a seance, and I know his brothers were there. I'm still murky on how it all works, but honestly, it sounds like Will kind of is, too. I guess it's something we'll figure out together, now that his wall thing came down, and he's already hearing spirits whispering right and left.

Across the table, Will clears his throat and I snap out of my thoughts. He's sipping his coffee, grimacing, and I shoot him a questioning glance.

"This is some weak ass coffee," he says with a sniff.

That gets him another eye roll, along with a chuckle. "Nothing's ever good enough for you, is it?"

Will shoots me a coy smile over his coffee cup. "I wouldn't say that. You certainly are."

"Jesus. How many times am I going to have to roll my eyes before this coffee's gone?" I'm acting annoyed, but I can feel myself blushing, and I know Will sees it, too.

"Who knows?" He smirks, reaching across the table to stroke my cheek with the back of a knuckle. "I like pissing you off. You're sexy as hell when you're mad."

"Huh. Noted."

I take a sip of my coffee, which is, in fact, *not* weak and makes me a little concerned about what kind of coffee Will's making at home. We've been spending most of our time together at my place, since Will's brother, Zeke, is still crashing at his place for the time being. Will said he wasn't ready yet to inflict his brother on me—which I found intriguing, although I didn't argue. After all, we have plenty of time ahead of us, and I want to savor every minute of it. Everything will come in time.

"Um…" Will runs a hand through his wavy mop of honey-colored hair. Meaning there's something he wants to bring up.

"Hey," I say gently, squeezing his knee under the table. "I'm listening."

He brings a nervous gaze to mine, but he clears his throat and continues. "So, you know Ethan Wilde, right? On the library board? Super successful developer here in Hawthorne Bay—and all over the greater Boston area, really…"

I nod. I'm more than aware of who Ethan Wilde is, of just what role he's had to play in this whole renovation business. And I know *Will* knows I know. But it's water under the bridge now. I won't hold it against the guy. I don't even know him.

"Right, so… he called me this morning. He's got that old colonial he wants to restore outside of town and up the coast a bit. Absolutely *gorgeous* property—original eighteenth century paneling, widow's walk, cupola, the works. And he wants me to design it."

Will stops, gazing at me. It seems like he's holding his breath to see what I'm going to say. It's like he thinks the very mention of Ethan Wilde is going to set me off. Like I won't be happy for him.

But nothing could be further from the truth. I'm fucking *proud*. Because I've also heard about this project—I don't think there's anyone in Hawthorne Bay who *hasn't*—and being chosen as the architect for something like this is huge. A career changer. And Ethan picked Will.

I meet Will's gaze, smiling. "You said yes—right?"

Will's taut face relaxes into a grin. "Fuck yeah, I did."

"Good. You better have." I take a sip of my coffee, give his foot a playful kick beneath the table. "But seriously, Will. That's... amazing. I'm proud of you, and I hope you know that."

He quirks an eyebrow at me. "Really?"

"Duh."

Satisfied, he settles back against the chair, arms crossed over his chiseled chest. I know I'm pretty much gawking at the way his biceps strain at his t-shirt, but *god*—would you blame a girl? I still can't get over how gorgeous Will Holloway is.

And I'm caught.

"Are you... checking me out?" Will's blue eyes sparkle as he feigns shock.

"No," I lie.

His lips curl into a devilish grin. "Uh-huh. Well, you know, there's still twenty minutes before I have to be back on site. We could—"

He's interrupted by the buzz of his phone, and I'm thanking my lucky stars. I cannot believe the shit he says in public sometimes.

Will answers his phone, and I sit sipping my coffee, watching him as he cocks his head to the side and listens to whoever's on the other end of the line. I'm trying not to listen in, but his expression when he answered looked so surprised I can't completely help it.

When he hangs up and shoves his phone into his front pocket, I resist the urge to ask who it was. But he can tell I'm curious. He wipes some imaginary crumbs off the table with a huge hand, then settles back against the chair again.

"My sister," he says. "I guess she was scrolling TikTok and lo and behold—there was our little brother, Zeke. Apparently, he's gone viral over the last few hours for some video... or reel... or whatever the fuck those kids put on there."

"TikToks. Reels are for Instagram."

"Okay," Will says, waving a hand. "Whatever."

"Well, what's the video?" I drain the rest of my coffee. "It's not... my mom's seance, right?"

"Hell, no!" Will looks absolutely aghast. "Are you kidding me? That shit is private. I'd wring his fucking neck."

I snort. "Okay. Then what?"

Will sighs, rubbing the back of his neck. "He made out with a ghost. It's *so* stupid."

I don't know what I was expecting him to say, but it was *not* that. I burst out laughing, and Will just looks at me a moment before letting the corner of his mouth hitch up into a half smile.

"Please don't tell me he made out with my—" I can barely get the words out I'm laughing so hard.

"You're absolutely disgusting," Will groans. But now he's laughing too. "And again, *no*. According to Phoebe, it was some ghost at the harbor—which checks out because he's mentioned it before. She said she'll send me the link, but I'm sure as shit not gonna watch it. I'd just as soon gouge my eyes out."

"But like... what does it *look* like? Can we see the ghost, too? Or just him? With his mouth all hanging open?" I'm half ribbing Will to get a reaction and half curious. Until last week, I didn't even believe ghosts were a real thing, so right now I'm in actual awe.

Will feigns a gagging noise. "I don't know, and I don't want to find out."

"You mean you haven't—"

Will cuts me off with a guffaw. "Jesus, woman! Save some mystery for later."

Pushing up from the table, he scoops up our coffee cups, and we head outside into the crisp, fall sunshine. Our coffee break is over, and we've got to head to the ground breaking.

As we crunch through the fallen leaves that pile on the sidewalk, I grab hold of his arm and nestle into his side. The early afternoon breeze is cool, but Will's body is warm and solid, and I swear to god there's never been anything sweeter than this feeling.

And then, because I just can't resist, I ruin the moment.

I look up at Will, a devious grin on my face. "Okay, but... will you *please* link me to Zeke's video?"

Will lets out a roaring groan, but throws his head back in laughter. We've reached the library corner, and he stops, grips my chin, and tilts my face up toward him. Then, right out in the open, he hits me with the most deliciously dizzying kiss.

"Fine. But don't say I didn't warn you—he's nowhere near as good looking as me." He pulls back, his fingers still clutching my jaw, and fucking *winks*. "And anyway, Lydia. You're mine now. Get used to it."

thirty-two

WILL

> Phoebe: So when do I get to meet Lydia?

> Will: She's in the truck with me. Just saw your text. Wants to meet you, too.

> Phoebe: Perfect! 😍

> Benji: Guys. Group chat.

> Phoebe: Oops. Sorry.

Everyone's already outside when we pull up at the library, gathered into a little cluster of hard hats and shovels. Lydia hops down from the cab, shielding her eyes as she surveys the tiny crowd of stakeholders. As we traipse across the lawn to join the group, all eyes are on us, and I see Nancy murmur something to the woman next to her, who I'm pretty sure is Hawthorne Bay's mayor.

No one says anything, but I can tell from the looks on their faces they're dying to know what's going on between the librarian and the architect. Showing up to the project ground breaking together, all smiles and coffee in hand, is a far cry from the verbal sniping we were doing in meetings just a few weeks ago.

Well, let 'em wonder. I'm still figuring it out myself.

"Will!" Ethan Wilde comes forward to shake my hand. He nods to Lydia. "Nice to see you."

"Likewise," Lydia says, giving him a quick little nod in return. She's still not Ethan's biggest fan—and I can't say I blame her—but she's trying, and that's what counts.

Nancy comes over and hands us a couple of hard hats. I swear, even with a shell of hard plastic on her head, Lydia's still so goddamn beautiful. Her eyes are dark and sparkling beneath the brim, and her hair cascades around her shoulders. I don't think anyone has ever made a hard hat look so sexy. Even though I know it'll only make the people here more curious, I reach out to stroke her silky hair. I can't resist.

"Now," Nancy says, clapping her hands together. "Before we start, we have a bit of an announcement."

Lydia's eyes flash to mine, and I shrug. I haven't heard anything about an announcement, but I'm instantly a little tense. We've come so far—thanks to her mom's reassurance, Lydia's finally feeling okay about the renovation—and I hope to god they're not going to throw us another curveball.

"Right," Ethan says. He scans the faces in our group, and his gaze lands on Lydia. "Before we break ground, we wanted to share that the board has officially approved a name for the new computer lab. It was important to us to honor the library's history, as well as acknowledge the central role it's played throughout the years in so many lives here in Hawthorne Bay. To that end, I'm happy to announce that today we're breaking ground on the new Sophia Chandler Media Center."

Lydia sucks in her breath. I see her lips move, like she's trying to parse what Ethan just said, and she knits her brow.

"Lydia," Nancy continues. "I know it's not what you originally wanted—but we wanted you to know how much the people of this town appreciated your mother, how much she is missed. We thought it was only appropriate that her memory be honored. A sort of tying together of the past and future, if you will."

"Thank you," Lydia says. She presses her lips together, blinking back tears. I wrap my arm around her shoulders and squeeze.

"And..." Ethan clears his throat, shoots me a meaningful glance that tells me everyone here's noticed that Lydia and I are more than friends. He hands Lydia and me each a shovel. "We also thought the two of you might like to do the honors of breaking ground."

Lydia takes the shovel from Ethan and grips it in her hands. This time, she grins. "You bet we would."

The small crowd gathers around us as we lift our shovels, waiting for the countdown.

"Threeeeee," Ethan calls, getting things back to business.

A photographer jumps out of nowhere and kneels down

in front of us, poised to capture the moment. The rest of the board members, along with Nancy and the mayor, all join in for Ethan's count. "Two! One!"

With a glance between us, Lydia and I dig the tips of our trowels into the ground and turn over a shovelful of rich, dark earth. Nancy whistles, and the rest of the crowd claps. A camera flashes and the photographer waves us closer together, holding up a finger to get us to hold our pose, then ushering more people into the frame.

Between photos with the mayor, the board, Ethan, and Nancy, I steal a glance at Lydia. Her eyes are sparkling, and she's taking in the moment. There's a sort of lightness around her now, a softness I had always sensed but could never really see. But now it's emanating from every fiber of her being—and she looks absolutely radiant.

For a second, I let myself tune into the ever present whisperings around me, let the voices start to come through. Lydia's mom isn't here now. Her business is finished, her work done. But this town's full of ghosts, in every sense of the word. After all, it's not just people who die. It's dreams, too. I know firsthand how broken hopes and ruined hearts can last for years, letting their darkness linger.

But for every shattered love, for every fractured ounce of trust, there's another kind of ghost—a spark of hope that flickers in the darkness. And those little sparks can last a fucking lifetime. They just need a little squinting to see, a little fanning to make them burst into something brighter.

Lydia beams at me, coming to wrap a slender arm around my waist. As she nears, the whispers grow louder—only for a second, before I tune them out again. The spirits in this town are always moving, always swirling, always sorting through their own unfinished business. And while I'm not running away from them anymore, I'm not here to make their troubles mine. I've got my own life to live. My own people to take care of. And that includes me.

But I think it's more than just Sophia Chandler who Lydia and I set free. From the crescendo of whispers I just heard, I'm pretty sure the spirits of Hawthorne Bay are celebrating with us. Here to honor the ones who've gone on, moved toward the light.

I'm drawn out of my thoughts when the sauntering, lanky form of my brother Zeke comes striding toward the library lawn. He's been strictly forbidden from getting behind the wheel of a car for several months, so lucky me has been carting his ass around. Today, I thought he planned to hang out at Brewed Awakening.

Well—no such luck.

Thankfully, though, the crowd has already dissipated, and the only people still standing around chatting are Nancy and the mayor. When Zeke whips out his phone and starts checking his reflection in the selfie cam, library building in the background, Lydia shoots me a curious glance. My reaction is the same as hers. What the hell...?

"Hey." I clap my hand onto Zeke's shoulder. "We're not quite done here. Give us five minutes?"

Zeke waves a hand at me. "Dude. You guys do your thing. I'm not here for *you*."

"Uh..." I'm at a loss. I also *really* don't want Zeke here, acting a fool around the mayor. "Who are you here for?"

"My *listeners*, Will. It's episode three of the Zeke

Holloway Haunted Experience podcast, and I'm taking my listeners on a live journey through one of the most haunted spots in town: the Hawthorne Bay Public Library."

"Oh, good god. Just what the world needs—a Zeke Holloway podcast."

"Love your attitude, bro," Zeke says, pounding my biceps with his fist.

He slips a pair of over-the-ear headphones on his head, gives his hair one last sweep of the fingers, and hits record. He moves away from me, now completely immersed in his own world, the excited notes of his voice falling into a steady rhythm as he launches into his episode.

"Starting a podcast, huh?" Lydia says, coming to join me on the sidewalk. A small smile plays on her lips as she looks up at me.

"Apparently."

"Well, maybe it'll be good. You *have* been wanting him to get a job, you know."

"Yeah—a *job*. This isn't a job."

Lydia smirks, her gaze following Zeke. "I'm not sure about that. You need charisma to be a successful podcast host, and if there's one thing Zeke's got, it's charisma."

"Ha. That's one word for it," I snort.

"Well, what else would you say? Charm? Magnetism?" Lydia casts me a wicked grin. "Allure?"

"Watch it, woman," I growl, moving my mouth to her ear.

Lydia laughs, and I draw her into my arms. Despite the chilly autumn air, her body's still warm, her cheeks still rosy as I pull her head against my chest and stroke her hair. I love this woman. I love the confidence she has in me, the faith she shows in my family—even my ridiculous, self-absorbed, head-in-the-clouds little brother.

"Can we go home?" Lydia asks. She looks up at me, her dark eyes soft and sparkling in the sunshine.

I give her one last squeeze before releasing her, threading my fingers through hers. "You've got it. Home sounds perfect."

WILL

Eight months later...

The front lawn of the library is already bustling when we get there. People are milling around with drinks, and the local folk band, whose lead singer Lydia says she went to high school with, is already strumming up a storm from inside the building. I hope to god someone tells them to take it down a notch before we get inside, or we won't be able to hear a goddamn thing.

Lydia tugs me along up the sidewalk. She looks back at me with a small smile, and I can tell she knows what I'm thinking. "The inside acoustics are much better now, remember? You'll live."

"I *know*. That's what I'm afraid of—it's going to be torture. Look at all these *people*."

Lydia shushes me, squeezing my hand. "Well, that's what you have me for."

"And also for this," I say, breathing the words into her ear as I give her ass a quick pinch.

She yelps, swatting my hand away with a grin. "William Holloway!"

Her head whips around to make sure no one saw the ass grab, and I pull her closer to my side, laughing. I can feel how warm she is, and I could bask all day in the sweet vanilla scent of her hair as it envelops me. I am so far gone for this woman it's not even funny.

People are already waving as we approach the front steps of the building, and someone—I don't even know who—claps me on the back. "Well done, Will! The place is magnificent."

And it is.

I can't help but steal a quick glance at the impressive exterior as we head inside, marveling at how my vision has come to life. I'm not the type to brag anyway, so I tend to keep my emotions under wraps when it comes to this kind of thing. But the fact that this building was the cause of so much hurt between Lydia and me still tugs at my heart—and I suspect it always will.

As though she can read my mind, Lydia squeezes my hand. It's her way of telling me everything's okay. That *she* is okay.

"Hey, you two love birds."

Lydia's friend, Autumn, struts over to us on her high heels, bag slung over her shoulder. She gives Lydia a peck on the cheek and then pulls back to look me up and down. "Your man's looking good, Lyds."

She winks at me, and I snort. I've gotten to know Autumn pretty well over these past eight months, and although she's always kind of been like this, her recent split from her douchebag husband has made her even more brazen.

Lydia just laughs. "Trust me—I know. Speaking of men, though…" She looks around dubiously, taking in the crowd around us.

Autumn shakes her head. "Nah. He's in New York, thank god. My guess is he's still miffed about having to give up the lake house, wanted to go off and lick his wounds by licking some—"

"Aaaaand that's my cue to go grab a Coke," I interrupt. I know how much Autumn means to Lydia, and honest to god, she's started to grow on me too. But that doesn't mean I want to hear about her ex-husband's exploits.

As I make my way to the makeshift bar they've set up on the far side of the foyer, I scan the crowd for any sign of my siblings. Phoebe and Benji are driving in from Boston, and Zeke should already be around here somewhere. He's still been living with me, which has made it difficult for Lydia and me to talk very seriously about moving in together.

But ever since that ghostly make-out session went viral, Zeke's been skyrocketing to internet fame—which, I can only hope, will mean *some* kind of income. With this new project I'm starting work on for Ethan, though, I'm less pressed about the financial side of things. I just want Zeke to get his act together. For his sake. And Lydia's and mine.

My hand drops to my pocket. Lydia and I may not have

our living situation entirely figured out yet, but I'm tired of waiting. I want Lydia completely, in every way possible, and I want to make sure she knows it.

My fingers close around the velvet box I slipped into my pocket before we left home. Before my mom died, she gave me her engagement ring—the one my dad proposed to her with. I was hesitant to take it, thought it might bring bad luck or something, but Mom refused to take no for an answer. She said that ring brought her the best parts of her life—us kids—and that it was up to us to imbue it with love again.

So I will. If Lydia agrees, that is. It's a simple gold band with a ruby in the center—oval-cut—and tiny diamonds clustered around on either side. It's understated, but classy as hell. Like my mom. Like Lydia.

Suddenly, Zeke's voice comes blaring at me over the din of the crowd.

"I mean... yeah. Everything we've got, they've got."

Christ.

He's at it again. He never shuts up about that video. About his podcast.

I get my Coke from the bar and follow the sound of Zeke's frat boy bragging to what looks to be a group of college girls crowded around him. He's got a drink in one hand, and he keeps swooping his hair back with the other while he works the crowd, his mouth curved into a sultry grin. And these girls are eating it right up. God help 'em.

"Who do I prefer? Now, that's a good question..." Zeke's saying, his expression turning thoughtful. "There're pros and cons, you know? Ghosts don't need the validation human girls need, but then again… it's the human girls you can really *grab*…"

I stride up to the group, clasping Zeke on the shoulder. I shake my head with a grin. "Honestly, little brother, I don't know how any girl would let you grab her after hearing this kind of shit."

"I would!" One girl pipes up, raising her hand like she's in fucking math class. She bites her lip, smiling sweetly up at Zeke.

"Oh hey, Will," Zeke says, running a slender hand through his hair again. He gestures toward the girl who just offered herself as tribute. "And to answer your question, *she* would. What's your name, babe?"

The girl holds Zeke's stare like it's a challenge. "Mackenz—"

"Okay, that's enough of that," I say, shoving Zeke away from the group and dragging him toward where I see Lydia and Autumn still chatting near the entrance. "Seriously, man. You're creepy as *hell*. You want to wind up on some neighborhood watch list?"

Zeke laughs like he's proud of himself. "Oh, come on, Will. She was 100% legal!"

"Who was legal?" Autumn asks with a smirk. Lydia's used to Zeke's antics by now—which she finds funnier than I do—and I can imagine she's filled Autumn in on a lot of them.

"You are," Zeke says, shooting Autumn a wink.

She snorts. "Oh, honey. I'm about a decade *too* legal for you."

Suddenly, a squeal erupts in my ear, and an arm loops

around my waist. We all whip around, and there's Phoebe, sunglasses pushed up onto her head and face beaming, with Benji right behind her.

"Will! This place looks *amazing*," Phoebe gushes. She's been down a few times to meet Lydia, but she's only ever seen the library from outside.

I'm not great with compliments, so I just nod. "Thanks."

"Yeah, way better than the last time I was in here," Benji quips as he comes in for a hug. I've been seeing more of him lately, as he's been coming down a couple times a month to sniff out the real estate market. He's thinking of opening a yoga studio, and I can't think of a better place for him to do it than Hawthorne Bay.

"Phoebe," Lydia says, her eyes lighting up. "You've gotta see the banister. Will heard how it was my favorite part of the building as a kid, and instead of replacing it, he worked the original into the plans and sharpened it up. It's magnificent."

She links her arm through my sister's, and the two of them take off toward the foyer. I sip my Coke, watching them leave, and my chest swells with happiness. I'm not surprised that Lydia and Phoebe have hit it off the way they have—they've both got snark to spare—but that doesn't make me any less grateful.

Autumn, who's been through the library a million times since the project wrapped and has already seen the banister, hangs back with my brothers and me. I can't help but notice that ever since his little comment about her age, she's been ignoring Zeke, but he's eyeing the crowd now and seems completely oblivious.

Autumn turns to Benji. "You're Phoebe's twin—Benji, right? The yoga instructor?"

"Yep," Benji says simply. It's not so much that he's *shy*—he's just a low key kind of guy.

"And you live in Boston?"

Benji shakes his long hair out of his eyes. "Sure do. Will keeps trying to get me to move out here and open a yoga studio, but I don't know. It's pretty quiet."

"Well, it seems like Will wishes it was a little *more* quiet around his house," Autumn says, shooting me a wink. She's right. I'm always complaining about what Zeke's getting up to. "Hell, if you moved out here, maybe you could take the poor orphan in. From what I hear, Will's place is nothing but pizza rolls and Axe body spray these days."

I groan like it's a joke, but I'm actually kind of annoyed. Our living situation is a sore spot for me. If it weren't for Zeke, Lydia and I would have been living together months ago. And anyway, Axe body spray? Really?

"Well, *you're* welcome to take in Little Orphan Zekey," I say, hitting Autumn with my most winsome smile. "I might even throw in a couple boxes of pizza rolls if you ask nicely."

She laughs, about to retort—and then stops. She looks at me, then at Benji, and then at Zeke. He's still scanning the crowd, no doubt trying to figure out where the 100% legal college chick wandered off to.

"Actually," Autumn says, her voice suddenly excited. "That's not such a bad idea. My lake house has a cabin on the grounds, where the caretaker used to stay. I'm not fucking around with any hired help, and honestly, it's just sitting there empty..."

"Wait, wait, wait," Benji cuts in. "You're not suggesting that Zeke moves onto your property... right?"

"That's *exactly* what I'm suggesting," Autumn says brightly. She snaps her fingers in front of Zeke's face, and he jolts back to face us. "Hey. You. You wanna live in my grounds cabin? Get out of your brother's hair?"

"Uhhh..." Zeke stalls, trying to orient himself in the conversation.

"Jesus, kid. Try to keep up." Autumn rolls her eyes. "There's an empty cabin on my property, and I'm asking if you want to move in there for a while. It'll get you out of Will's hair, Lydia will stop bitching about having to sleep apart from Will, and there'll be a dude around to protect little old me if anyone tries to break into the grounds. Honestly, it's a win for everyone."

Benji shoots me a questioning look, and I shrug. I've got my doubts, but I'm thinking about the box in my pocket. If all goes well... the idea of finally being able to share a space with Lydia is tempting. I'm already imagining us bustling around the kitchen together and spending lazy Sunday mornings in bed. Hell, fucking on the living room couch if we feel like it.

Phoebe and Lydia appear behind my shoulder, just as Zeke asserts a resounding, "Fuck yes."

"If what I think I just heard is correct, Autumn, my heart goes out to you," Phoebe says. "And also you're crazy."

"I know I am," Autumn says, smiling proudly.

Next to me, Lydia grins. She whispers something into Phoebe's ear, and my sister snickers. I have no clue what they're gossiping about, but the fact that Lydia fits so well into my family is seriously the stuff of dreams. For a guy who's spent the better part of his adult life ashamed of where he comes from, I never *dreamed* a woman like Lydia Chandler would show up and fit right in. That she'd take the parts of me I spent so long trying to shove out of sight and somehow turn them into something beautiful.

It's a fucking miracle, honestly.

And that's when I know it's time. The velvet box is burning a hole in my pocket, and despite the fluttering of my stomach, I know this moment is the right one.

Placing my hand on the small of Lydia's back, I guide her out to the foyer. She shoots me a questioning look, but she lets me lead her, the gentle twang of the music drifting along with us. When we reach the banister, I turn to look at her, sliding my hand from her back to my pocket.

She's looking up at me curiously. "Everything okay?"

"Yeah."

"Are there too many people? Do you need to take a minute—"

I drop to my knee, and she stops. I can tell by the look on her face that she knows what's coming, and it makes my heart beat that much faster. We've only talked about this once—a couple months ago—and then I tabled the subject, frustrated by the situation with Zeke, with our living space. But I'm going to take the leap. And I'm hoping against hope that Lydia will take it with me.

"Lydia," I say.

Her voice is breathless as she stares at me, cheeks slightly flushed. "Yes?"

"I've been trying forever to figure out the best way to do

this—and I don't fucking know. You know me. I'm not good at this."

Lydia's silent, but I can see her lips twitching, like she's holding back a smile. It makes me grin, and something in my chest loosens. I can do this. *We* can do this.

"The one thing I do know," I continue, "is that I want to spend the rest of my life with you. Brother or no brother, your house or my house—I don't fucking care. I just need you with me."

I pause, drawing the velvet box out of my pocket and flicking it open. I hold Lydia's gaze, and the warmth of her cinnamon eyes is downright intoxicating. "So I want to know, Lydia. Will you marry me?"

Lydia gazes at the ring a moment, then brings her eyes back to mine and pulls me to my feet. She draws me toward her and stands on her tiptoes to kiss me, then pulls back and grins.

"Absolutely, Will. Abso-fucking-lutely."

Something lets loose inside my chest, and I pull Lydia toward me, my hand on the back of her head, my mouth hungry for hers. I'm just pulling her hips into mine, getting ready to slide my hand down to grip her ass, when applause erupts from the doorway and I freeze. Lydia snickers as we turn to see my siblings and Autumn, all standing there grinning.

"You better have said yes," Autumn calls, hand on her hip.

"Her loss," Zeke jokes, and Phoebe elbows him.

Leave it to this crowd to not give us a moment of privacy, even during a damn proposal. I can't help but chuckle, though. It's such an accurate representation of our lives right now—and somehow, just like this impromptu proposal, it works for us.

Lydia and I head back up the stairs, holding each other close, and our little crowd of family gathers around us. The girls want to see the ring, Zeke wants to know if he needs to pack up his shit, and everyone's all smiles. It's everything I've ever hoped for.

As we head back inside to rejoin the party, my mother's ring now sparkling on Lydia's finger, I stop near the doorway, close my eyes, and listen to the bustle of the community around me—just for a second. The library building may not look exactly how it used to, but it's full of life again—and I think Sophia Chandler would've wanted it that way. I think my soon-to-be wife knows that, too.

The chatter of friends and the lively small talk of the town echoes through the hall, underlaid by the strumming of the folk band. And underneath it all, there's a steady hum, a constant pulsing of energy. I can't see the spirits—they're hanging back, overwhelmed by the hordes of people drifting through the place—but I can feel them in my chest. Hear their silken whispers rustling in my thoughts. And for the first time, maybe in my whole life, I'm thankful for them.

As Lydia leans into my side, resting her cheek against my chest, I hold her close. This woman brought the darkest parts of me to light. And it's in this moment I realize...

My heart's not haunted anymore.

I'm home.

want more?

Join my newsletter for an exclusive bonus scene where Will and Lydia's spicy time gets interrupted by ghosts. I'll also send you a free prequel novella!

To get the bonus scene, scan the code below or head to lucyvalebooks.com/bonus-signup.

about the author

Lucy Vale is a tarot reader, former ghost hunter, and unapologetic Halloween fanatic who loves a good spooky story—especially if it comes with a happily ever after.

Originally from small-town Nebraska, she's now lived in four different countries, but always ends up coming back to the places with the best autumn weather.

She lives with her husband (who insists he's never seen a ghost) and their daughter (whose supernatural abilities are still TBD).